# Clearing the Course
## *A Sugarbury Falls Mystery*

by

Diane Weiner

For information, email Cozy Cat Press, cozycatpress@aol.com or visit our website at: www.cozycatpress.com

**COZY CAT**
**P R E S S**

ISBN: 978-1-946063-56-4
Printed in the United States of America

10 9 8 7 6 5 4 3 2 1

This book is dedicated to my wonderful readers.
Thank you for supporting my writing.

Chapter 1

Emily struggled to keep her jet-lagged eyes open as she rocked in the passenger seat of her husband Henry's Jeep. She'd trotted all over the country in her career as a crime reporter, but now that she was in her mid-fifties, teaching at St. Edward's College and writing true crime books was more her speed. She let out a yawn, which she'd been stifling throughout the memorial service.

That poor young girl. Dead. She'd sat in the pew behind the girl's parents. The mother smothered her tears in her husband's jacket sleeve. The father gripped his wife's hand—a life raft in a violent sea. Shuddering, she looked in the rear view mirror at Maddy, asleep in the back seat, and waited to see her breath rise and fall before turning to her husband.

"Henry, no one said how Damari died."

"I found that strange, too. Your guess is as good as mine."

"Car accident?"

Henry shook his head. "She didn't have a car. She walked a long way to get to work. Heard her say more than once how she hated getting all sweaty before her shift started." A blond head popped into his rearview mirror.

"Are we there yet?" said Maddy. "Do we have to stay long?"

Teenagers. At least they weren't afraid to say what they were thinking.

"We can't run in and run out. Henry worked with poor Damari and her parents are hurting badly. You saw them falling apart at the church." As soon as the words left her mouth, she questioned her own sensitivity. Maddy's wounds from witnessing her own mother's funeral were recent enough to be raw.

Henry said, "I'm sure her parents regret the day they agreed to let Damari move to Vermont. If she'd stayed down in Miami, they wouldn't be burying their daughter."

Emily's stomach ached. If anything ever happened to Maddy... She'd been wrong in assuming most of her life that she lacked maternal instincts. Maddy had only been with them a little over a year and she'd fight like a lioness to keep her safe.

"How long did she work at the hospital?" asked Maddy.

"She started working reception in the ER last summer. When the semester began, she cut back to part time." Henry chuckled. "I didn't think she'd make it past that first day. Must have been a full moon the night before. A screaming toddler with Skittles stuck up his nose, a lady blowing up before her eyes from an insect bite, and a husband demanding Damari look up whether his insurance covered out of state emergencies while his wife bled all over the floor—Welcome to summer in Sugarbury Falls. Had to give her props for not quitting before lunch."

Henry turned into the parking lot in front of the yellow inn with the white wrap-around porch. "Here we are." He read the hanging, wooden sign aloud. "Coralee's Outside Inn, the finest establishment in all of Sugarbury Falls."

Emily pulled down the visor and checked the mirror. She had her roots done right before the trip but already spotted white strands peeking through her auburn hair.

"Come on, girls. Let's get the show on the road."

Maddy stumbled out of the back seat, repositioning her blond ponytail. "I want to check on the cats, first."

"Maddy, don't you think…"

"That's fine," said Henry. "I'm sure they've missed you." He turned to Emily. "She can do that while we catch up on the details." Maddy ran ahead and Henry whispered, "We may have to soften the news when we find out the details of Damari's death."

They walked under a canopy of lush shade trees and up the white wooden porch steps. The front door was propped open. Coralee, directing traffic in the lobby, said, "Everyone's in the dining room. I'm sorry you came back to such a sad event. How was Scotland?"

"Wonderful. We officially renamed the castle 'Fiona Manor' in honor of Maddy's mother and made a memory garden out back." Emily wished they could have done more to ease Maddy's loss. "Coralee, how did Damari die?"

"Well, there are a few theories floating around…" Another group came into the lobby and Coralee shuffled them all into the dining room.

Emily heard muffled bits of conversations as they made their way to Damari's parents. She caught the words 'mysterious' and 'puzzling' as she passed through. Mrs. Cooper, a Viola Davis look-alike, wilted against her husband. Mr. Cooper gripped his wife's hand like a vice, as he had earlier at the church. Emily flashed back to her sister's funeral and how her own father held her mother, blanketed in grief, unable to stand.

"Mr. and Mrs. Cooper, we're so sorry for your loss." The emptiness of those words always bothered her but she'd never found an acceptable alternative. What can you say to someone whose heart has been forever scarred?

"Thank you," said Mr. Cooper.

"She was a ray of sunshine. We're so sorry," said Henry.

"Skiing. That's the real reason she wanted to go to college in Vermont you know." Mr. Cooper looked Henry in the eye. "How did you know our daughter?" he asked.

"I worked in the emergency room with her."

"Yes," said Mrs. Cooper. "She was happy from the day she was born. It's...it's so...so upsetting that...what people are saying." She sobbed into her husband's shirt.

"We're Catholic. Suicide is a sin." Mr. Cooper pulled out his handkerchief.

Mrs. Cooper lifted her face from her husband's shirt. "And there's no way it was an accident. Damari was an expert rower. She was on the crew team all through high school." Anger in her voice momentarily overrode the grief.

Emily tried to piece together the snippets she'd heard. Rowing. So she must have drowned. They'd flown in from Edinburgh late last night and she hadn't gotten a chance to call her friends or check the newspaper. Why was it a memorial service and not a funeral? Especially if they were Catholic? She suspected the police weren't ready to give up the body. They made their way over to Pat, the medical examiner and Henry's best friend.

"Pat, what's going on here?" asked Henry.

"Welcome home, buddy. You missed the drama. Damari's body was found floating in Lake Pleasant the morning after the big Founder's Day celebration. According to her parents, she was an excellent swimmer."

"Had she been drinking?"

"I didn't find any traces of drugs or alcohol in her system. The boat was recovered, undamaged. No signs of a struggle."

"What's your detective girlfriend think?"

"Megan says they're investigating. So far, that's it."

Emily saw Damari's parents talking to Coralee in the corner. Coralee's son, Noah, circulated with platters of finger sandwiches and chips. A large man about Henry's age approached.

"I didn't know you guys were back from Scotland. We missed you at work."

Dan Fisher was an ob-gyn and often crossed paths with Henry and Pat at the small, local hospital.

"Scotland was beautiful," said Henry. "My daughter inherited her very own castle."

"I meant to congratulate you the last time I saw you. Coralee mentioned the adoption is final now."

"Yep. Never expected to become a dad in my fifties, but better late than never."

"Heck, look at those Hollywood types. George Clooney's got twins and he's older than you. At least you're not waking up nights to feed her."

Emily said, "Do you have children, Dan?"

"Me, no. Thank God. Two ex-wives, my salary goes right to alimony. Imagine if I had to pay child support on top of it."

"Dan, do you know what happened to Damari?"

A young couple carrying soft drinks in their hands, nearly ran into Dan.

"Dr. Fisher, so sorry. Nothing spilled on you, did it?"

Dan put his arm around the petite, ebony-haired woman. "No, sweetie. Not a drop. Henry, Emily, Pat, this is Li Min Weng and her husband, Shen."

Li Min blurted out, "I hope we'll be seeing you regularly, Dr. Fisher." She turned to Emily. "Dr. Fisher is helping us get pregnant."

Pat and Henry stifled snickers, but their faces displayed their amusement.

"Sorry," said Shen. "Sometimes the nuances of English still challenge us. What she meant to say was that Dr. Fisher is supervising fertility treatments for us."

Emily found it odd that they would blurt that out to virtual strangers, but she could see the excitement in Li Min's face. "Are you friends of Damari's"

Li Min's expression sullened. "Yes, good friends. I can't believe she's gone. We saw her at the picnic and the last thing she said was that she'd see us at the fireworks that night. I looked for her, but she never showed up." She wiped a tear with her hand.

Pat said, "A fisherman spotted her body floating in the lake the next morning."

Dan said, "I left early. Got called to the hospital."

Pat cleared his throat. "There was a note. On her computer…"

"No." said Li Min. "The note wasn't referring to suicide."

"With all due respect, no one but the detectives know what the note says," said Pat.

"She did look a little upset," said Dan.

"I thought you left early?" Emily grabbed a drink from a silver tray being circulated.

"I did leave early, but I ran into her before that, while we were in line for hot dogs. She looked as though she'd been crying."

"Like Megan always says, you've got to look at all the evidence before you start speculating," said Pat. "Speaking of Megan, I need to get going. We're driving over to Oakbridge for dinner."

Dan said, "Excuse me, too. I want to pay my respects to Damari's parents. Looks like they're getting ready to leave."

After the two men left, Li Min said, "There's no way she killed herself, and no way it was an accident. It was that miserable boyfriend of hers. He murdered her."

Emily ran through what she'd learned. Damari could swim and row. Dan said she looked upset. She never showed up at the fireworks, and there was a note on her computer, which Pat implied was a suicide note. No evidence of a struggle, as far as what Pat said. And she wasn't drunk or high. The boat was undamaged, and her best friend thinks she was murdered.

A young man wearing jeans and a red *No Fracking* t-shirt barged into the dining room, as if on cue. He knocked food off the tables and stammered into the center of the room.

"Why wasn't I invited? No one thought to tell me? My girlfriend dies and I'm not invited to the funeral?" He slurred the words together. Emily thought he was on the verge of losing his balance. Luckily, Coralee's son made his way over to him.

"Come on, bro. Come into the other room and I'll get you some coffee," said Noah.

"I don't want coffee. I want Damari." He stammered back to the door, guided by Noah.

Li Min said, "See what I mean? That's Damari's ex-boyfriend. That's Robby, the no good son of a..."

Shen put his arm around her. "Come on, you don't want to get upset. It's bad for the baby."

Emily saw Li Min's expression soften. Should her husband be getting her hopes up like that? She knew infertility treatments were often unsuccessful, yet he was talking like she was already pregnant.

"I'm feeling kind of tired. It's been a stressful day," said Li Min. She followed Shen out the door.

"Well," said Henry. "Let's get Maddy and head home, unless you want to stay longer."

"Nope. I'm ready. Take us home."

Chapter 2

The next morning, Chester 's persistent nudging and meowing left Emily with no choice but to get out of bed. Henry moaned and pulled the quilted comforter over his head.

Emily slipped her feet into her terry scuffs. *Like Chester ever had an empty bowl*. Grumbling, she made her way down the loft ladder to the kitchen and topped off his dish with Feline Feast. The store brand was cheaper, but Chester refused to eat it. Maddy, in pajama pants and a t-shirt, plopped down at the table. When Chester saw her, he jumped up on her lap, ignoring his breakfast.

"How were the café cats doing?" She'd been so tired last night she hadn't even asked.

Maddy said, "All the ones who were there before the trip were adopted, except for the two black ones, and the one with the missing patch of hair."

"Looks matter, even when it comes to pets. I didn't give a second thought to Chester's color until Halloween rolled around that first year and I saw a story on the news warning viewers to keep their black cats indoors 'for their own safety.' Not that I 'd ever let him outside anyway."

Maddy grabbed a granola bar from the pantry. "Why was Robby yelling in the dining room at Coralee's? I meant to ask you last night."

"You know that young man?"

"Robby Birchfield. He cleans rooms at the inn and he's really good with the cats."

"Is he new in town? I'd never seen him before."

"He came here for school. He goes to St. Edwards. I'm surprised you never ran into him."

"St. Edwards is small but not so small that I know everyone. Anyway, stay away from him."

"Why would you say that? You just said you don't even know him."

"He was drunk and totally inappropriate barging into the dining room like he did. And he's a murder suspect."

"Robby? No way. He loved Damari. When she broke it off, he was sad, not angry. You're so judgmental." Chester jumped down and ran into the living room.

"How do you know he wasn't angry? You heard him at the inn yesterday."

"He stopped by the cat café a lot the week before we left for Scotland. He was trying to cope with the fact that Damari already had a new boyfriend. He isn't a murder suspect."

Henry, bringing a plate to the table, grabbed a cup of coffee mid-brew. "Who's not a murder suspect?"

"Emily thinks my friend Robby killed Damari."

"That's not what I said. What I said was…"

Henry interrupted. "Let's not put the cart before the horse. Who says she was murdered? Pat's the medical examiner and he's still considering suicide or an accident."

Emily popped frozen waffles into the toaster. Yet again, Henry the peacemaker; her, the enemy.

"What are you lovely ladies doing today?"

To Emily's surprise, Maddy said, "I was hoping Emily could take me to the mall."

Emily wondered if she meant take her as in *shop with her*, or take her as in *drop her off*. The mall wasn't right around the corner and Emily didn't relish making two round-trips.

"One of the girls from my class is having a quincenera next week and I need a dress."

"Sure. I didn't realize Sugarbury Falls was so multicultural. Which friend?"

"Bianca from school. You don't know her. And that comment is racist."

"Racist? I was simply saying…"

"What's a quince-whatever anyway?" Henry poured himself a bowl of Corn Flakes.

"She's turning fifteen."

"So, it's like a sweet sixteen party," said Emily.

"No. She's turning fifteen." Maddy glared at her, sarcasm in her voice.

Henry considered this progress. When they first brought Maddy home she had been overly polite, but now she had no qualms about expressing herself. He never had a sister, but he remembered his cousin talking like that to his aunt when they were growing up. Mothers and teen age daughters were supposed to be adversarial. He'd read that in one of their parenting manuals.

"This vacuum packed almond milk is like water. I'll run by the grocery store after my golf game."

"Since when do you play golf?" They'd been married thirty years and she'd never once heard him mention playing golf.

"My Dad and I hit the driving range a few times growing up." Henry mimed swinging a club. "I'm hoping it's like riding a bike. Dan Fisher was talking to Pat and me yesterday and suggested getting together. That new course by the lake just opened up last week. I'll be a few hours at most."

They heard a knock. "That must be Kurt," said Henry. A scruffy man with a Minnesota Vikings jersey balanced a bundle of newspapers and mail under one arm and gripped a leash in the other. Henry bent down to pet the black lab. "How's it going, Prancer buddy?"

Kurt followed Henry into the kitchen and dropped the bundle on the table. "Here you go. Two weeks-worth of mail and newspapers." He let go of the leash, and Prancer ran over to Maddy, tail wagging, tongue hanging out like a stretch of taffy.

Emily handed him a cup of coffee. "Thanks for taking care of things while we were gone."

"Nonsense. That's what neighbors do. How was England?"

"Scotland. It was beautiful. Guess we missed out on some excitement here, though."

"You mean the murder?"

Maddy piped up. "Henry said it's not murder."

"I said it hasn't yet been determined. Damari Cooper's ex-boyfriend made quite a scene at Coralee's yesterday. Some kid named Robby. Do you know him?"

"Robby Birchfield? Yeah. Nice kid. I hired him to help me clear out the dead trees behind the cabin I bought for Chloe. Hard worker."

"See," said Maddy, glaring at Emily.

"What kind of scene? Can't imagine him causing trouble."

"He came into the dining room, ranting about not being invited to the memorial service. I think he was drunk." Emily sat at the table.

"He doesn't drink," said Maddy. "He's a vegan and doesn't put garbage in his body."

Emily wondered how Maddy knew so much about this boy. Until now, she'd never mentioned him, yet they seemed to have spent time together. He had to be half a dozen years her senior.

Prancer barked. "He wants to continue his walk," said Kurt. "Welcome home."

Henry said, "Maddy, what *other boyfriend* did Damari have?"

"Some old guy. Robby saw them having a picnic together."

"I'll bet he was jealous," said Emily.

Maddy jumped to the rescue. "What? And killed Damari over it? No way."

"She's right." Henry sipped his coffee. "He'd have gone after the boyfriend instead."

Maddy exhaled through gritted teeth and stormed off to her room.

Emily said, "I wonder if the police know about this older boyfriend?"

"Are you talking about detectives Megan O'Leary and Ron Wooster? Sugarbury Falls finest? They won't leave any stones unturned."

"Hope not. I'm going to get ready." She straightened the pile of papers and mail Kurt dumped on the table before going upstairs. *Nod your head and don't give any opinions on the dresses unless she asks.* She thought back to the battle she and Maddy had last time they shopped.

Henry drove to the golf course early in order to rent clubs before meeting Pat and Dan. His father, also a physician, had loved golf. Henry foraged through the barn hoping he'd find a set of clubs his dad stashed away before he died, but had no luck.

Henry was relieved when he saw Pat already in line. "You don't play either?"

"Nope," said Pat. "Just wanted to be social and check out the new course." He pulled out his credit card and handed it to the cashier. When they finished, Dan was waiting outside.

"You're going to kill us, you know," said Pat. "You understand that Henry and I don't play golf, right?"

"It's about bonding. I hardly play myself, but this course just opened and I sort of got the itch."

Henry had to admit it was the perfect day to be outdoors. After spending the past two weeks in chilly Scotland, the sun felt good on his face. The grass had been mowed to perfection and the view of Lake Pleasant was like something out of an art museum.

"They sure transformed this run-down farmland," said Pat. "These acres had been neglected ever since the owner died." He took a slow breath. "Smells like the pine cologne Megan got me last Christmas."

Dan placed his ball on a tee, swung, and missed. Several times. Henry relaxed. Maybe he wouldn't have to claim an old shoulder injury after all. While Dan was a poor golfer, both Henry and Pat were abysmal. When a foursome pulled up waiting to play the hole, they graciously let them play through.

"Third time's a charm."

"You mean sixth time," said Henry.

"Yeah, but who's counting." Dan again put his ball on the tee. This time, he connected on the first try, but the ball went off the course, into the trees by the lake. "I think I saw where it went," said Dan. "I'll be right back."

"This was a terrible idea," said Pat.

"Ah, the weather's nice and it got us away from work. Think he'll find that ball?"

"I don't know why he bothered going after it. Hey, here he comes."

Dan, panting, held a dirty, red lunch box. "Didn't find the ball, but I found this in the clearing by the lake."

"Why are you holding that dirty thing?" said Pat.

"Because I found it just feet away from the yellow crime scene tape. I'll bet it belonged to Damari Cooper's killer."

Chapter 3

As much as it bothered Henry to have paid for and not fully utilized both the tee time and the clubs, the threesome cut their game short. He looked at his Fitbit. *I put in more steps making coffee and reading the paper than I did here.*

Pat called Megan. "Hey, we found something at the golf course that you should see. We're on the way over." They caravanned to the police station.

The modern police station in the center of town looked out of place amongst the older brick stores and restaurants. After the original station caught fire several years ago it was rebuilt using an updated, streamlined design. Henry wondered if all the original buildings would disappear in time, leaving Sugarbury Falls devoid of its history.

Megan and her partner, Ron Wooster, met them at the entrance.

Using his golf towel, Dan handed them the lunch box and they followed Megan into her office. "It was right outside the crime scene tape, under a fallen branch and covered by twigs and dirt. I brushed away the leaves, looking for my ball, and I found it."

Megan, pulling her curly red hair off her face with a rubber band, donned gloves and unzipped the lunch box. "It has initials written in Sharpie. *RB*."

"Robby Birchfield!" said Dan. "What's in there?"

Megan pulled out a syringe. "This is interesting. I'll get it to the lab right away."

"Do you think Robby drugged her and that's why she fell overboard?"

"We can't jump to any conclusions. We'll run all this through the lab and go from there."

Ron Wooster said, "I'm surprised the team didn't find this when they investigated the crime scene. How could they have missed it?"

Dan said, "It was outside the yellow tape, and if I hadn't been clearing away the brush to find the ball, I'd never have seen it myself. Don't be too hard on them."

Megan said, "When I interviewed the hospital employees the other day, you said Robby Birchfield took care of your lawn. Had you ever seen him using drugs, or did his behavior ever imply such?"

"Well, I hired him on occasion when I was too busy to mow my own grass. I never really thought about it, but now that you bring it up, he did seem a bit off a few times. Never to the point where he wasn't able to do the job, but I guess it's possible."

Henry worried that Maddy would be upset at the very mention of her friend being implicated. "Megan, we were out of town when Damari's body was discovered, but our daughter says she and Robby were friends. He worked for Coralee as well. Do you want to talk to Maddy?" He still tingled when he said the word *daughter.*

"Absolutely," said Megan. "Do you mind bringing her over later?"

Pat said, "We're driving right past your house later on our way to see the summer stock production at St. Edwards. If it's okay with Megan, we can stop by and she won't have to hang out any longer here than she has to."

Ron said, "That's fine with me. Otherwise, I'll stay and interview her here."

Megan sealed and marked the evidence bag, then peeled off the gloves. "No, it shouldn't take long. We'll be by around 7."

When Henry got back to the cabin, Maddy and Emily had returned from the mall and were huddled over Maddy's laptop.

"That was a quick golf game. You must be better than you thought you were."

"No, Em, I was more awful than I imagined. We had to make a detour to the police station. Dan found a lunch box with a syringe in it over by the crime scene while chasing a lost ball. It belongs to Robby Birchfield."

"What!" said Maddy. "How do you know it's his? Do the police think he's guilty now?"

"Well, why would he have been near the crime scene with a syringe?" said Emily.

Maddy huffed. "He's diabetic. Maybe he carried around emergency insulin, even though he has that Pod thing he wears. Robby is the gentlest, most peace-loving man I know," said Maddy.

Emily was convinced Maddy had a crush on this boy. Wouldn't that color her judgment?

Henry said, "Megan's going to stop by around 7 to talk to you. Tell her what you told us. Meanwhile, what are the two of you so engrossed in on that laptop?"

Emily said, "When Megan stops by, maybe she can help solve another problem."

"I checked my Facebook. Mostly I use Instagram, but I keep in touch with one of my old teachers from Chicago that way. Read this."

*I wish I could be happy. They're right. I'm useless and ugly.*

"Who wrote that?" said Henry. "Your old teacher?"

"Oh, no. Some friend I don't even remember having. She calls herself Feo. I think she's alluding to the Spanish word for ugly. It gets worse."

*I couldn't get out of bed all day. I can't go back to that school. I want to die.*

"That's serious," said Henry. "You can't figure out who it is?"

"No. It's so frustrating. I'm going to ask Megan about it. Maybe the police can find out who she is."

"The poor girl is crying out for help. Did you reply and try to find out who she is?" Henry asked.

"Of course, Henry. I said she could private message me and I want to help her but she didn't answer."

"Why don't you just run through your friends list?"

"I asked her that," said Emily. "This person has over 600 friends on Facebook." She was confused as to how someone with 600 friends could feel unloved.

Maddy closed the computer. "I'm going to ride my bike over to Coralee's and check on the cats. I'll be back before dinner."

"Don't forget, Megan will be here at 7 so in case she's early…"

"Yes, Emily. I'm not stupid. I said I'd be back by dinner." She slammed the door on her way out.

Henry put away the bag of groceries he'd picked up and offered Emily a Diet Coke.

"Did you buy any chips? It's that sort of a day."

"I got us a bag of Baked Lays. Semi junk food. How was the mall?"

"We found a beautiful dress for the party. Maddy looks so much older when she's dressed up and not running around in those ripped jeans. I told her I'd take her to get her hair done for the party."

"I'm sure she loved that," said Henry, sarcastically. He knew how much Maddy resisted anything that made her 'artificially pretty,' as she put it.

"No, I was as surprised as you were. She liked the idea. On the way home, she was flipping through pictures of hairdos on her phone. Oh, and she wanted to step into Sephora while we were at the mall."

"What's that?"

"They sell cosmetics. I bought her a light pink lip gloss. It's a start."

"Start of what, I'm afraid to ask. Do you think she has a boyfriend and isn't telling us?"

"I don't think she has a boyfriend yet, but she's warming up to the idea. She's fourteen. I guess it's normal." Emily tried to sound confident.

"I'm keeping an eye out. What if she goes for that Robby character or someone like him? He's a college kid and she's a freshman in high school."

"She's nearly a sophomore, but I agree with you. She has to stay away from older men."

"Damari's parents should have taught their daughter that. Maddy says Robby told her he saw Damari with 'some old guy.' I hope it isn't what got her killed."

Chapter 4

Megan and Pat arrived right at 7. Megan looked elegant in a lacy white sundress and Emily marveled at what a touch of makeup did to bring out her blue eyes. *She'll make a lovely bride if Pat ever gets his act together and proposes.*

"Maddy," called Henry. "Megan and Pat are here." Maddy plopped down on the sofa.

"What are you doing during your summer vacation?" asked Pat. "Other than your Scotland vacation."

"I'm going to spend time at the cat café. I'm helping Coralee come up with an expanded menu."

"You mean like Lion Claws? You know. Instead of Bear Claws. Those fried things with the powdered sugar…" Pat gave up.

After a bit of chit-chat about the adoptable cats, Megan pulled out a notepad. "Maddy, how do you know Robby?"

"He cleans rooms for Coralee. One day he wandered into the cat café and we started talking. After that, he came by to play with the cats whenever he could."

Emily wondered if the cats were really the draw. She'd bet dollars to donuts he was stopping by to see Maddy. Henry's clenched fists told her they were on the same wavelength.

"Did he talk about Damari Cooper? Did he mention the nature of their relationship?"

"She was his girlfriend, until she broke up with him. They took some classes together at St. Edwards."

"Did he say why they broke up? How did he react to the separation?"

"He thought she was seeing someone else—an older man. He was heartbroken, poor Robby. She was an idiot to let him go."

"Did he know who the man was? Was he angry at Damari?"

"He wasn't angry. He blamed himself for not being a good enough boyfriend, though I can't imagine it. He thought the guy might be a professor. Said he had that look."

Megan cleared her throat. "Did you ever see evidence that Robby used drugs?"

"Drugs? No way. He was into health big time." Maddy shifted in her seat.

Emily and Henry sat up straighter. Megan nudged her on.

"He was diabetic, you know. Not the kind you can fix by cutting out sugar. He had this thing attached to his arm."

"An insulin pump?"

"He said he used to have a pump, but this was newer and didn't have wires. He called it a Pod."

Megan scribbled notes. "So he may have syringes and insulin, right?"

"I never saw him with a syringe."

Pat looked at his watch. "We should get going if we want to get to the show on time."

Megan closed the notepad. "Thanks, Maddy. If you think of anything else, call me."

Emily nudged Maddy with her eyes. Unsuccessful, she took it into her own hands. "Megan, Maddy has something else to ask you about."

"Sure, anything."

Maddy walked to the door with her. "I've been seeing these weird posts from someone I don't remember at all. She keeps saying how sad she is and…she needs help. Can you trace Facebook and find out who she is?"

"No crime has been committed, correct?"

"Yeah."

"Then I'm afraid there's not much we can do. Why don't you see if you can draw out some information from her, convince her to get help? You can post the 24 hour National Suicide Prevention number. It's 1-800-273-8255. Does she post pictures? Sometimes you can learn a lot about someone from the pictures they post."

"I didn't see any pictures, and there's no info on her profile page."

"Sorry I can't be of more help. Keep me in the loop, and if you remember any other details regarding Robby…"

"I'll call you."

After Megan and Pat left, Emily said, "Anybody want a cup of tea?" She wished she'd have put pound cake and chocolate syrup on the shopping list.

"Tea?" said Maddy. "Since when?"

"I don't know. I kind of got used to it over in Scotland. Henry?"

"Sure, I'll take some." He pulled out the Sudoku from the morning paper. "Want a copy, Maddy? We have two weeks-worth waiting for us."

"No, I want to finish my book." She scooped up Chester and went into her room.

Emily pulled the cabinet door open. The knob fell off, and the latches came loose. "Henry, can you help?" The door fell into her hands.

"What's wrong?" When he saw her holding up the ancient cabinet door, he said, "It's time we redo those cabinets like we talked about. They're the same ones that we had when we spent summers here as a kid."

"I'll ask around for suggestions. Didn't Pat redo the cabinets at his place a few years back?"

"Yeah, when his wife was alive. I think her brother did it for them. Let's not go there." Henry unscrewed the latches and propped the cabinet door against the wall. While the kettle boiled, he and Emily sat at the table.

"I forgot we had that hot cocoa Susan and Mike sent us for Christmas. I'm going to see if Maddy wants some."

When she got to Maddy's door, she heard voices. At first she thought Maddy was on the phone, though that was a rarity. She pressed her ear against the door. Maddy was talking to a boy. Should she swing open the door? If Maddy had a boy in there, surely she'd have locked the door. She scooted back to the kitchen.

"Henry, come quick. Maddy has a boy in there."

"No way." He followed her to Maddy's door and pressed his ear against it. "I'm going to go around back to the window. Give me a few minutes, then knock. This way he can't escape."

Emily counted. *One Mississippi, two Mississippi...* She pounded on the door. "Maddy, open up!"

"Just a minute."

Emily heard shuffling, then the sound of the window slamming down. Emily opened the door. Next to the window, trapped between her and Henry, stood a boy with black hair and a red t-shirt. Emily recognized him immediately. It was the uninvited guest at the memorial gathering. It was Robby Birchfield!

Chapter 5

Henry pushed Robby onto the bed. Emily's heart raced. She was surprised, angry, confused.

"What's he doing here!" She sounded like a lunatic sitcom mom, but didn't care.

"It's not what you think."

Emily focused on Henry's angry, bulging forehead veins. "Then explain." He towered over Robby, who was slumped on the edge of the bed.

He needs our help," said Maddy. "He has nowhere else to turn."

"Where are his parents?"

"Emily, they're divorced and don't care. His mom's in and out of rehab, and his dad is always traveling for business."

Henry interrogated the boy. "They found your lunch box and a syringe. What was it doing near the crime scene?"

"I have no idea. I lost that lunch box; I can't even remember when. Used it when I did my lawn jobs and had to be outside all day. As far as the syringe? I don't use them." He touched his upper arm. "This pod delivers my insulin. Sure, I'm supposed to keep a few needles on hand in case of emergency, but I don't."

"And you did a lawn job by the crime scene?"

"No, never."

Emily said, "Where were you the day of the picnic?"

"Home alone, mostly. I grabbed a corn fritter earlier, but left way before the fireworks started."

"Did anyone…"

"See me? Did I have an alibi? No. I went home and watched a game on TV. It's not like I have any friends here, except for Maddy and she was in Scotland."

Emily looked at Henry, reading his thoughts. She knew Henry would do anything for Maddy, including helping her questionable friend. Who was she kidding? She wasn't about to leave Maddy and this pitiful kid on their own either. What kind of parents must he have to think he can't even depend on them?

"Is he going to be arrested?" asked Maddy.

"They'd need something more tangible. I doubt the forensic tests have come back already, and if he says he wasn't anywhere near the crime scene, a lunch box alone is flimsy evidence." Henry sat on the bed. "Just to be prepared, I'll look around for a lawyer. You try to think if anyone at all can vouch for your whereabouts. Did you pass a neighbor? Order pizza? Get gas? Think hard."

"I don't think so."

Emily said, "How about Henry takes you home?. Get some rest and don't panic yet."

Maddy's face softened and Emily read the relief in her eyes. "Thank you for helping him."

"We haven't done anything yet. Hopefully we won't have to." Henry grabbed his keys and led Robby to the car. Maddy followed Emily into the living room. "Did you say something about tea?"

Emily had forgotten the now whistling kettle, which barely contained enough water now for tea. She grabbed tea bags from the cabinet and plucked them into the new mugs they'd acquired on their trip. Robby would probably need a lawyer. Who did she know who practiced law? There was the guy they used when Uncle Malcolm threatened to take Maddy away, but this wasn't his field of expertise. Henry might know someone through the hospital. Criminal law...She had a flash. Her friend from when they lived in New York. Susan Wiles's father was a lawyer. He'd been retired but then stepped forward when Susan needed him.

"Emily, can you bring in the biscotti with the tea?"

Emily tucked the box of forgotten biscotti under her arm and carried the tea into the living room. "My friend, Susan Wiles from back in Westbrook, has a father who's a criminal lawyer. If need be, I'll contact her and see what we can arrange."

"But he lives in New York. Can he close up shop just like that?"

"He's retired, so maybe."

Maddy sipped her tea. "I'll bet on my life that Robby didn't have anything to do with the murder, if that's what it was. You should see him with Cocoa at the cat café. He doesn't have a mean bone in his body."

"Someone once said that anyone is capable of murder given the right circumstances. If he felt betrayed by Damari…"

"No way. He was really upset when she broke up with him, but was trying to move on."

"Sounds like the two of you are close. You know he's a lot older than you."

"We're just friends." She crossed her arms over her chest. "We get each other. That's all."

By the time they'd finished their tea, Henry was back.

"I want to help the kid, but something doesn't add up."

"So you think he killed Damari? Seriously?"

Henry sat next to Maddy on the sofa. "I didn't say that. I just think there's something he's not telling us. The police haven't even determined it's a murder yet, so why is he acting so guilty?"

Chapter 6

The next morning, Emily went for a run, made difficult due to her two-week hiatus.

When she turned the corner, she ran into Kurt and Prancer.

"Missed seeing you out here. No one to share theories with over the murder."

"Why is everyone calling it a murder?"

"You know these small towns. By the way, I saw Henry driving that Robby kid around last night."

"If it turns out to be a murder investigation, I'm afraid he's the prime suspect."

"Him? I can't see it. More likely that old guy she hangs out with."

Emily wasn't sure she'd heard him right. "What old guy?"

"Prancer and I have been taking longer walks now that the weather's nice. Twice I saw the girl at the picnic table down by the lake with a gray-haired gent. His back was to me both times, but I saw the hair. They held hands over the table last time."

"Did you tell the police? And when was the last time?"

"Let's see, it was…the night before the Founder's Day picnic. Yeah. It started sprinkling, so Prancer and I sorta jogged back home."

Emily couldn't imagine Kurt, with the build of a Minnesota lumberjack, jogging, but that was beside the point. "You have to talk to Megan."

"I didn't think it was important, but I guess I can stop by the station."

"Please do."

\*\*\*\*\*

Henry stopped by the morgue before his shift in the ER. He couldn't imagine working in the sunless room surrounded by dead bodies every day, but Pat was very much at home here.

"Hey, buddy. Any news on Damari's case?"

"I ran the tests again. No sign of drugs or alcohol."

"What about insulin?"

"Her blood sugar was in the normal range. If insulin is all forensics finds in that syringe, then it's not the murder weapon."

"You're calling it murder?"

"The police don't want it released, but let me show you something." He walked over to the autopsy table. "See this bruising around her stomach? She couldn't have done this by accident."

"The shape. Did someone hit her with a tennis racquet?"

"Something heavier. Someone knocked her into the water with an oar, is my guess."

"Did the police find the murder weapon?"

"Not yet, but when I was out with Megan last night, she got a call from Detective Wooster. Someone called the tip line. They saw someone with a red hoodie running away from the shore the night of the picnic. His build fits Robby Birchfield's."

"Maddy will be upset. Do you know that boy snuck into her room last night! She says they're friends and he's estranged from his parents. Maddy's spot on when it comes to reading people and she's sure he's innocent."

"He snuck into her room? Seriously?"

"Yeah. A regular Romeo. She says he was upset about breaking up with Damari, but not angry. And Robby said he lost that lunch box weeks ago, probably while doing a lawn job."

"Insulin didn't kill her, so they have nothing tying him to the murder scene except the lunch box."

"How many murderers have you heard of who carry lunch boxes to a murder scene?"

Pat covered Damari's body and led Henry into his office where he checked his cellphone. "It's a message from Megan. We're supposed to meet for lunch." He made a face as he read the text. "Looks like lunch is off. A biker found a red hoodie by the lake. Megan has to go follow up."

"Want to grab something in the cafeteria later?"

"Sure. Call down here when you get a break."

Henry's head hurt when he saw the number of patients waiting in the ER. A summer flu bug was making the rounds through a near-by summer camp and although he'd been at this a long time and had the immune system of an elephant, he was occasionally caught off guard. *The last thing I need is to get sick right now after being out for two weeks on vacation.* He donned a mask and wove his way through the cubicles. Two hours later, his stomach growled and his headache worsened. Ready for a break, he found himself in line at the cafeteria, where he'd agreed to meet Pat.

"That wrap doesn't look half bad," said Pat.

"Turkey on spinach tortilla, no mayo." He picked up a crinkled bag from his tray. "And baked Lay's. Have you tried these, they're not half-bad?"

Pat grabbed one of his own cheese smothered French fries. "No thanks."

"Isn't that Dan over there with the loaded tray?"

"I don't see any seats."

Pat called to him, "Hey, want to join us?"

Dan sat down across from Henry and said: "Delivered two babies this morning, back to back. Usually get maybe one a month. Must have been a full moon."

Pat said, "Finished up the autopsy on Damari Cooper."

"What did you conclude?" Dan bit into his cheeseburger.

"Let's just say I ruled out suicide, and accidental death is looking unlikely," said Pat. "Your girlfriend have any leads?" Ketchup dripped onto his chin.

"An anonymous tip identified a boy in a red hoodie running away from the crime scene the night she died. A biker just found the hoodie," said Dan.

"Are they arresting the boyfriend?" asked Pat.

"Who says it's Robby Birchfield's hoodie?" asked Henry. Why did he feel he had to defend this boy? Maddy. She swore he was innocent. He didn't relish proving her wrong.

"I just thought," Henry said, "since someone spotted a boy in a red hoodie fleeing the crime scene…"

"Red's a pretty common color for a hoodie." Pat chomped on another fry, wiping orange cheese sauce off his hand with a paper napkin.

"It would be hard to connect the two," said Henry. "And if red is his favorite color, or they were on sale at Walmart, heck, the whole town could own one." That made him feel strangely better.

"The kid should find himself a good lawyer." Dan gulped his coffee.

"Why do you say that?" said Henry, hoping for Maddy's sake it wasn't true.

"Red hoodie, lunch box with his name at the crime scene, ex-girlfriend," said Dan. "Besides, what enemies did she have? She was sweet as pie. Everyone at the hospital loved her."

"He's right," said Pat.

Henry took a bite of his wrap. If he got dragged into helping Robby for Maddy's sake, the first thing they needed was more suspects. Who else wanted Damari dead?

Chapter 7

While Kurt went down to the station to report seeing Damari with a gray-haired man, Emily drove over to St. Edwards College. Henry hadn't yet returned from the hospital. She herself had taken the summer off, but her friend Nancy was teaching a class and Li Min, Damari's best friend, worked in the housing office. Maybe they could identify the man Kurt saw Damari with and suspicion wouldn't fall solely on Robby.

Nancy, always with a smile, said, "Hey, what're you doing here? You're supposed to be off this summer."

"I know, but I'm trying to help a friend of Maddy's. You know the girl who died a few days ago?"

"Damari Cooper. Of course I do. She was a student here you know. I never taught her, but my friend who teaches in the science department knew her. She was a Bio major."

"Are you finished for the day?" Emily looked at the pile of papers on her friend's desk and was glad she'd taken the summer off.

"Yeah. I was just going to look over these essays, but I was considering doing it by my pool."

Emily's phone vibrated. "It's Maddy. What's wrong? Questioning? That doesn't mean he's under arrest. I'll be home soon."

"Is Maddy okay?"

"They brought her friend in for questioning. He was Damari Cooper's ex. Hey, do you suppose your friend from the science department is here?"

"Yes. She's teaching summer semester. Want to meet her?"

"If you don't mind. I'd like to go back to Maddy with a sliver of hope."

Nancy locked her office, then led Emily out the stone building, across the cobblestone path to the science building. Although a few students were scattered around, Emily felt the campus looked creepily deserted. Nancy knocked on her friend's office door. The placard said Dr. Dinnerstein.

"Come on in. Done for the day?" The professor was slightly older than Emily and Nancy. Emily put her around sixty.

Nancy said, "This is my friend, Emily Fox. She works in my department and wanted to meet you."

"I'm flattered. What can I do for you?"

"My daughter's friend is the prime suspect in Damari Cooper's murder. Mainly, because no one else seems to have motive. Damari was spotted down at the river with an older, gray-haired gentleman. I was wondering if you knew who that might be."

"Damari Cooper. What a dear. She had a promising future ahead of her. Was aiming for med school and I have no doubt she would have gotten in. Such a shame."

"Did she ever mention anyone to you who meets the description?"

"We didn't talk about her personal life. I prefer to keep my relationships with students professional. Unlike some of my colleagues."

Emily's adrenaline started flowing. "Anyone particular in mind?"

"Professor Carlson, over in Biology. He has gray hair and Damari was close to him. She was doing research and he supervised it. Saw them together on a number of occasions."

"Is he working this summer?"

"Yes, but not every day. I didn't notice his car in the lot. He's got this over the top Mercedes and he always takes up two spots like he's entitled."

Emily said, "Thanks for the information."

"Hope it helps."

Emily walked Nancy to the parking lot, then went across the street to the housing office. She hoped she was on to something, and quickened her pace. When she got to the housing office, Li Min was sitting at the counter sorting mail.

"Can I help you?"

"Li Min? We met briefly at the memorial service the other day. I'm Emily Fox."

"Yes, now I remember you. You and your husband were talking to Dr. Fischer."

"That's right. I understand you and Damari were friends."

"Best friends. I know that sounds odd, given I'm a decade older than she is—was. She lived in the dorm next door and we had this instant connection." She pointed out the window.

Emily saw her discreetly wipe a tear with the sleeve of her sweater. "Do you have any idea who may have killed her?"

"The police asked me that. No. I don't know of anyone who didn't like her. She'd do anything for anyone."

"What about Robby Birchfield?"

"They broke up, but I know Robby wanted her back. If he didn't kill her, I don't know who did." Li Min sipped a green shake, making a face. "This tastes awful, but it's supposed to be good for the baby."

"Congratulations! I didn't know."

"Well, we aren't sure yet, but we've been working with Dr. Fischer on our infertility issue and I'm positive this time it took."

"I wish you luck. Children are a blessing." A year ago those words never would have made it past her lips. She never wanted children. Not since she felt responsible for her own sister's death. Not since her parents divorced and her mother went off the deep end. If her college roommate hadn't died and named her guardian, Maddy never would have come into their lives. She shuddered thinking of what she would have missed.

"Did you ever see her with a gray-haired gentleman?"

"Only Dr. Carlson. He was her advisor and supervised some research she was doing."

"Was it more than professional?"

Li Min laughed. "Half the girls in his department have a crush on him."

Emily probed further. "After Robby, was Damari seeing him, or anyone new?"

Li Min blushed. "She was seeing someone, but she didn't tell me who it was. She wanted to keep it secret."

"Professor Carlson?"

"I didn't say that. I really don't know. Whoever it was, it was a new relationship and Damari wasn't ready to talk about it." A student came to the desk to pick up a package. "I should get back to work."

Emily walked back to her Audi. An older man with gray hair, a secret new relationship, Professor Carlson... Maybe things were looking up for Robby Birchfield.

Chapter 8

When Emily opened her front door, Maddy ran to her, half shrieking, half crying. "You've got to do something. How could they? Did you call a lawyer? He's in jail."

Henry stood behind her. He tried to put his arms around her but she pulled away.

Emily knew before she asked. "Did they arrest Robby?"

"Y-Yes. You have to help."

Henry said, "They found a red sweatshirt near the crime scene next to a fast food receipt that they traced to Robby. Robby says it isn't his but a witness saw someone fitting his description running away from the lake the night of the picnic. And his fingerprints were all over the lunchbox."

"He explained all that!" shouted Maddy. "And it's not his hoodie. Was it missing the drawstring? Robby's is missing the drawstring. Can you get a lawyer?"

Emily said, "I did some digging. There's a gray-haired man who was seen with Damari. Sounds like the professor she was working with. And her friend, Li Min, says she was seeing someone new, just like you said."

"Did you tell the police?" Maddy paced across the living room.

"Not yet. I just found out." Emily pulled her phone out of her purse. "I'll call my friend, Susan, and see if her father is available." She sat on the sofa, praying Susan had her phone on.

"Is she answering?" said Maddy.

Emily nodded. "Hello, Susan. Great to hear your voice, too. I'm hoping you can help us. Maddy's friend has been arrested for murder. No, I'm not asking you to come solve it. Yes, you trained us well. Do you think your father would be willing to drive up and help him out? Really? Okay. We'll talk soon. Call me as soon as you find out? Great."

Maddy grabbed her arm. "What did she say? Is he going to come?"

"She'll call him and get back to us. Meanwhile, Henry, can you think of any other lawyers in case he can't do it?"

"I don't know any criminal lawyers, but I'll call the guy who handled Maddy's adoption. Maybe he can recommend someone."

"Can you drive me to the police station?" asked Maddy.

"No, honey. They aren't going to let you see him now."

"Can you at least call and tell them about the gray-haired man?" She reached down and scooped up Chester, rubbing her face in his shiny, black fur.

"Of course." Emily picked up her phone and dialed Megan's number. When she finished, she reassured Maddy that the detectives would look into it. She walked into the kitchen, opened and closed the fridge. Then she foraged through the cabinets. Another knob broke off in her hand, reminding her to find someone to install new cabinets. "Do you want to go to Coralee's for dinner?"

Maddy said, "How can you think about food right now?"

"Coralee knows everybody in this town. I'll bet she knows Damari's professor." Emily's phone rang. "Susan, that was fast. Really? Tomorrow? Tell him thank you; that's a big relief. I'll set him up with a room at Coralee's place. Should we pick him up somewhere? He's driving. Okay. Thanks again."

"He's going to do it?" said Maddy.

"Yes, and while we're at dinner, we can book a room for him. I don't know how long he'll need to be here."

"Go wash your face, Maddy and let's head over." Henry grabbed his keys.

By the time they pulled up to the yellow inn with the white shutters and wrap around porch, Emily's stomach was rumbling. She'd been on the go all day and had neglected to eat lunch. She hoped Coralee had the squash casserole on the menu as well as her prize-winning apple strudel.

"How's the little family doing tonight?" asked the pudgy owner with the sparkling eyes and rosy skin. "Maddy, those cats, I swear they know when you're coming. They were all up at the door of the café waiting for you."

"I'm going to say hello before dinner."

"Remember to wash your hands afterwards," said Emily. When Maddy rolled her eyes at her, she wondered if she should have just trusted her and not said anything.

Coralee led them to a table. "I heard about poor Robby. There's no way that boy's a killer. He's a hard worker and so polite to everyone. I'm sure it's a big mistake. He and Maddy had gotten pretty friendly. How's she taking it?"

Emily said, "She's hysterical over it. I have a lawyer coming in tomorrow from Westbrook. Remember Susan and Mike, the ones who helped clear Noah? Can you book a room for him? We'll pay for it."

"Nonsense. If he's coming all this way to help that boy, the room's on me for as long as he needs it."

Immediately, Emily noticed her favorite dish listed under the specials. Coralee had made a real effort to add vegetarian meals to the menu ever since Maddy came to town. While waiting for dinner, Emily reminded herself to ask about someone who could install new kitchen cabinets. It'd be expensive, but they were sorely needed. Perhaps she should have taught that summer course after all.

Coralee brought squash casserole, pasta primavera, and chicken fricassee to the table. "Maddy's coming. I told her dinner was ready."

"Smells great," said Henry. He already had his fork in hand.

"Coralee, do you know anyone who does cabinet work?"

"If you want it done over the summer, Dallas Peterkin might want the extra work what with a new baby and all. He did some work for me last summer, before he and Lisa headed home, and I've got him putting shelves in the second floor rooms this summer."

"I remember him. His wife was pregnant."

"Yep. And baby makes three. That cabin they bought is going to be a tight fit in a few years. It's only got one bedroom and one bath."

Maddy came to the table. "Coralee, can we get into Robby's room to get him a change of clothes and a toothbrush?"

Emily knew the jail wouldn't allow it, unless Megan could pull a few strings.

"Sure, honey. After you all have a proper meal," said Coralee.

"I didn't know Robby lived here," said Emily.

"He cleans the rooms and does all sorts of odd jobs for me. Besides, he's a broke college student. I don't mind giving him a hand."

Emily gobbled down the casserole and was the first to ask for the dessert menu. She needed to get back into a fitness routine soon or she'd turn into a blimp. Running helped curb her stress; without it, she ate instead.

"Can we go to Robby's room now? I'm done," said Maddy.

Henry scooped the last bit of ice cream from his sundae dish. "I'm ready." He waved to Coralee.

"He's in here." Coralee unlocked Robby's door. "Just grab what you need. The police may be upset if it turns out they need to search his room and I've let people in."

Maddy opened a drawer and fumbled through the clothes.

"What are you looking for? Just grab something quick," said Emily.

"It's the sweatshirt. I can't find it."

"Maybe he was wearing it when the police picked him up." Emily grabbed a toothbrush from the bathroom. The police found a sweatshirt and Robby's was missing. Trying not to connect those dots, she grabbed Robby's brush. Maddy held up a razor.

"Seriously, Maddy? Even if Megan can smuggle in a toothbrush, a razor is considered a weapon."

"Leave it?"

"Leave it," said Henry.

Maddy opened the closet.

"Maddy, you ready?" said Henry.

"I'm looking for a pair of slippers and his flannel shirt. I'll bet it's drafty in jail." She moved the suitcase out of the way. "Emily, Henry, come quick! I found something."

"What?" said Emily. She could see that Maddy was upset.

"It's…it's…"

"What?" said Henry and Emily, practically in unison.

"Don't tell the police."

"Tell them what? Let me see." Henry moved into the closet. "You've got to be kidding."

Emily wanted to push them both aside and see for herself, given the anticipation they'd created.

Henry said, "Get me a towel, Maddy." Then he stepped out of the closet. In his hand, he held a wooden oar.

Chapter 9

The next morning, Emily and Henry waited anxiously for Jonathan Stirling, the lawyer, to arrive. After giving the oar to the police the previous night, Emily called Susan and explained that the potential murder weapon had been found in Robby's closet. Given the urgency, Jonathan Stirling agreed to get a few hours of sleep, then drive straight through to Sugarbury Falls.

"Maddy, did you sleep at all?" asked Emily. "Let me make you some eggs."

"I can't eat. What time will the lawyer get here?"

"He's going straight to the jail. He'll call when he gets there. For now, there's not much you can do."

Henry said, "Maddy, you have to brace yourself. The murder weapon was found in his closet. It's not looking good."

"You don't know it's the murder weapon. Did they find blood? Or Robby's prints?"

"Haven't heard yet, but Pat's the medical examiner and based on the bruises on Damari's stomach, he thinks she was hit with an oar, and pushed into the water where she drowned. Besides, there was a stain on the oar."

"I don't believe it. Someone planted it there to make Robby look guilty."

Henry put his hand on her shoulder. "The room was locked. Surely Coralee didn't plant it there and she's the only one besides Robby who had a key."

Maddy said, "Let me know when the lawyer's here."

Emily hugged Henry as soon as she heard the inevitable door slam. "It's looking dismal for Robby, isn't it?"

"You mean besides having the murder weapon in his closet?" he said. "He was the murder victim's ex. His lunch box, with a syringe inside, was found near the crime scene. Someone called the tip line and reported seeing a boy who fits Robby's description, wearing a red sweatshirt by the way, leaving the crime scene the night of the murder. And the police found his red sweatshirt on the path down to the lake."

"There's no proof it belongs to Robby," said Emily. "Maddy says his was missing a drawstring. Did the police check that? We didn't see it in his room." She prayed Maddy was right.

"And the oar in his closet?" asked Henry.

"Why would he be dumb enough to bring the weapon home with him? Why not throw it in the lake, or bury it in the woods? It's too neat. Besides, Maddy is convinced he's innocent."

"I know. And I trust her instincts as well." He looked at his watch. "I have to go to work. Call me after you talk to the lawyer."

Emily poured food in Chester's bowl, and sat down to finish her coffee. There *was* another suspect. The gray-haired man. Presumably Professor Carlson. She was drawn to her laptop, and retrieved it from the table, spilling a bit of coffee as she tripped over scraps of dismantled cabinet.

Emily started with his faculty bio on the school website. He'd been at St. Edwards for the past fifteen years. Before that, he was at Yale. Yale? Why would he leave there to come to a small liberal arts college like St. Edwards?

Maddy came into the living room. "I was checking my Facebook, and that girl posted again. I think she's going to kill herself. She says she's been stealing her mother's sleeping pills and almost has enough to do the trick. Can't the police intervene?"

"Megan said they can't. But I know who might have a different answer. And, who might know something more about a certain professor. Who do we know who runs around wearing a Yale sweatshirt?"

"Rebecca! She's a techno nerd. Let's go over there."

Sitting around waiting for the lawyer to call felt like watching paint dry. Emily stuck her phone in her pocket, grabbed the keys, and said, "Let's go."

The morning sun was obscured by clouds as she and Maddy walked the short distance to Rebecca and Abby's wooden cabin, nearly identical to their own, but lacking the master bedroom loft. Emily's head ached from the heavy air which promised a thunderstorm later in the day. They found Rebecca pulling up weeds in front of her cabin.

"Hi, guys. Out for a walk?"

"We came by to see you. We need your expertise."

Maddy bent down to pet Milo, the couple's black and white Border Collie.

Rebecca shook the dirt off her hands as best she could, then invited them in.

Emily loved the hominess of their place, and had borrowed several of their ideas while redecorating. "Where's your wife?"

"She's doing a photo shoot. Engagement pictures. Hope the weather holds up." She washed her hands in the kitchen sink with a squirt of Dawn. "Want a drink?"

"No, thanks." She got right to the point, hoping she didn't sound rude. "Maddy's friend, Robby, has been arrested for killing Damari Cooper."

"Really? I didn't know they were calling it murder."

Maddy said, "He didn't do it. He's being set up. Emily has an idea."

"Kurt spotted Damari with a gray-haired man down by the lake. Damari's friend says she was seeing someone new. We think it's her professor, Simon Carlson. We were hoping you could dig up some background."

"He taught at Yale, and you went to Yale. Can you find out why he left to come here?" said Maddy.

"I'll give it the old college try. Get it?"

Emily's phone vibrated. "Mr. Stirling? Okay. We'll talk to you afterwards."

Maddy said, "Is the lawyer here?"

"Yes. He's about to go in and talk to Robby. He'll call us afterwards."

Rebecca had already gotten onto the Yale website. "He was gone before I went there, but I'm checking out some of my professors who may have been there when he was." She tapped her short nails on the keys. "Here's one. I had Dr. Shepard. She was old when I was there. She told us she'd proudly been there her whole career. Want me to try her?"

"Sure," said Emily.

"I'll start with her, then go through these names and see who else may have worked with him. Do you know if he's married?"

"No." Emily checked her phone, hoping Jonathan had texted.

"I'll dig up some public records and whatever else I can find."

"That's great. Also, Maddy wants help with another problem. Can you trace someone who's on Facebook?"

"She writes these sad posts and I think she's going to kill herself," said Maddy.

"That's a tough one. Are you sure she's not just seeking attention?"

"More like she's crying out for help."

"I'll see what I can do. Forward me the posts."

Emily moved toward the door. "We're going to head back. We're waiting on pins and needles to hear what the lawyer has to say after talking to Robby Birchfield."

Maddy gave Rebecca a hug. "Thank you."

Chapter 10

Shortly after arriving home, Emily put on another pot of coffee and took a loaf of banana bread out of the freezer. "Maddy, are there clean towels in the bathroom?"

"I'll check."

Emily swept the kitchen floor and took plates out of the cabinet with the broken handle. Keeping her hands busy stopped her from checking for messages every few minutes. Finally, a call. Jonathan Stirling was on the way. She wiped off the table and threw the rag under the sink.

"Maddy, come on. The lawyer's on the way."

Maddy joined her, tapping the table and staring at the rooster clock. In the anticipatory silence, every click of the minute hand made her jump as they sat waiting for a knock.

"Emily, I hear a car outside." Maddy ran to the door.

Emily took a deep breath, smoothed her humidity swollen hair with her hands, and pulled the door open. Her heart fell, looking into the wrinkled face of a man who looked more like a nursing home resident than a lawyer.

"You must be Jonathan Stirling." She knew that sounded stupid. Who else would he be? The Fuller Brush man? "Please come in."

He towered over her as he shook her hand, then Maddy's. His nails were well manicured, and his gold watch understated. She invited him into the kitchen.

Expecting more of a slow shuffle, she was surprised at how gracefully he moved.

"Thank you so much for coming up here, and so quickly," said Emily.

"My schedule is rather flexible. Besides, I love practicing law. It keeps me young."

Maddy said, "How's Robby?"

"Worried, tired...but I think he feels better now that we've started strategizing."

"What's your plan?" said Maddy, hands on hips.

"I want to prove Robby's alibi is legit. Perhaps a neighbor saw him, or someone out for an evening jog. Then, we make a list alternate suspects to introduce reasonable doubt in case we wind up going to trial."

Emily said, "Our neighbor, Kurt, says he saw Damari holding hands with a gray-haired man down by the lake. And Damari's best friend says she was seeing an older man. I think it's a Professor Carlson. Simon Carlson."

Jonathan opened his brief case. Pulling out a legal pad, he said, "How do you spell the professor's name? And here, write down the names of the best friend and your neighbor. We'll start there."

A knock at the door startled Emily. "I'll get that." When she opened the door, she saw Rebecca standing in front of her, laptop cradled in her arms.

"I think I found something."

"Come on in." Emily introduced her to Jonathan. "Jonathan, this is our neighbor, Rebecca. She's a whiz at technology." *And spying and hacking into private databases.*

Rebecca shook his hand. "Nice to meet you. Look, I found out Professor Carlson left Yale mid-semester before moving to Sugarbury Falls. His wife died of cancer, and there were rumors going around that he hurried things along."

Emily felt encouraged. "That was quick!" She read the obituary over Rebecca's shoulder.

Jonathan said, "This professor works here now?"

"Yes, at St. Edwards, where I teach part time."

"Has your neighbor identified this Professor Carlson as the man he saw with Ms. Cooper?"

Emily said, "Well, we haven't asked yet. Should we go over? He lives right on the other side of our barn."

"Let me get up to speed, first. The victim, Damari Cooper, was a college student and worked at the hospital, correct? That's what my daughter Susan told me."

"Yes. While we were away in Scotland, the town celebrated Founder's Day. There was an all-day picnic/barbecue at the park by Lake Pleasant."

"And she was at this celebration? There were witnesses?"

"Yes. Dan Fischer, a colleague of my husband's, says he saw her there."

Maddy said, "And Robby told me she had a new boyfriend. An older man."

"Kurt saw her with a gray-haired man at the picnic tables by the lake. At the service, someone mentioned a note, possibly a suicide note," said Emily. "I'd almost forgotten about it."

Jonathan jotted down the information. "I'm going to drop by and see the professor after I get situated."

"You can follow us to the Sugarbury Outside Inn. I made you a reservation. I think you'll find it comfortable."

Rebecca said, "I'll call my contact at Yale and see what else I can dig up."

Emily and Maddy escorted Jonathan to the inn. Any reservations Emily had about Jonathan's advanced age had dissipated after spending time with him. He was sharp as a tack, just like his daughter, her good friend, Susan Wiles.

After getting Jonathan settled, Coralee said, "I want to introduce you to Dallas Peterkin. He's doing work on the second floor right now. Come on."

"I'm going to check on the cats," said Maddy.

"The litter boxes are getting nasty," said Coralee. "You remember our deal?"

"Sorry, Coralee. I'll do it now."

Coralee took Emily up the back stairway, which creaked with each footfall. One of the guest rooms was propped open with a paint can and a dark-haired gentleman hammered shelves into the closet. Curly black hair peeked out from the back of his Yankees baseball cap. When he turned around, Emily recognized him right away.

"Emily, this is Dallas Peterkin."

"Yes, I remember you from last summer. You're the history teacher, right?"

"That's me. And you're the doctor's wife."

"Great memory."

"When my wife fell and hit her head last summer, your husband ran some tests. Sent her home with a clean bill of health."

Coralee said, "Dallas is a new father. Their baby was born a few months after they left last summer."

"Congratulations. Boy or girl?"

"A precious little girl. Alexandra Sophie."

"Are they here with you?" Emily remembered speaking to his wife on several occasions.

"Yes, at the cabin we rent every summer."

"Let me see a picture. Babies are so precious."

"I left my phone in the car, but I have plenty."

Coralee said, "Emily is looking for someone to do cabinet work. I recommended you."

"Thanks. I can use every extra bit of money I can get now that there's another mouth to feed. I'd be happy to come by and take a look after I finish here."

"Great. We'll be there. Coralee will point you in the right direction."

Emily stopped at the cat café. The cat condo, which started as a simple cat tree, had been expanded even further than it was last time she'd seen it. It now connected to a wrap-around shelf near the ceiling which circled the entire room. Two customers sipped coffee at one of the tables Henry built. Emily bent down to pet a calico, lying on its side in a cushioned cat bed.

Maddy held an oversized orange tom-cat. "Litter is changed. Did you see the basket of books Coralee put by the rocker? She said customers donated them and they all feature cats! One is all about a high school girl who starts a cat café as a community service project."

"Sound like your very own biography. Ready to go?"

After leaving the cat café, Emily headed home, excited at the prospect of new cabinets. She changed her clothes and relaxed with a cup of tea and a book. Maddy plopped onto the couch.

"Don't you think that lawyer is really old? I think we need someone born in this century."

"He's got a lot of experience and he's smart as a whip. I trust him."

"Do you think he knows how to use a computer?"

This time it was Emily rolling her eyes. "Seriously?"

After a while, Rebecca called.

"Emily, I did some more digging. Professor Carlson had charges brought against him for domestic abuse. It was long before his wife got ill, but it shows he's got the capability."

"Did the charges stick?"

"No. His wife withdrew the accusations."

"What else did you find out? Why was he suspected in his wife's death?"

"She'd made it to church the evening before her death and stated in front of the congregation she wished God would take her before the pain got worse, or that he'd give courage to a loved one to help her move on. She died the next day while she was alone with Professor Carlson. A vial of morphine was missing. One the pharmacy has just filled."

"How did you get all that so fast?"

"My old professor. She exhausted what she knew, then gave me a few more names to talk to. Hope it helps."

"I'll call Jonathan right away. You're amazing."

Maddy said, "There's another suspect, right? Do you think they will let Robby go now?"

"It's going to take some more work before Professor Carlson is a viable suspect. We don't have any physical evidence placing him at the picnic. Not yet, anyway."

Emily finished her tea and was about to start a load of wash when there was a knock at the door. The dark-haired teacher/handyman from the inn stood holding a tool box.

"Dallas. I almost forgot you were coming by. Come on in."

"Cute cabin. Very homey," said Dallas, as he followed her into the kitchen. She wished she'd taken the time to wash the breakfast dishes piled in the sink.

"As you can see, the cabinets aren't in great shape. Henry's parents owned the place, and before that, his grandparents. I think these might be the original ones."

Dallas opened the doors and jiggled the knobs. Then he ran his fingers over the brass latches. "The wood's warped and all the hardware needs replacing. I think you're better off starting from scratch rather than trying to repair these. I can build you some new ones for a reasonable price."

Emily weighed Henry's woodworking skills against the offer Dallas made. Henry was a perfectionist and she estimated how long it would take him to do it, with working part time at the hospital. Dallas had a built-in deadline. He'd have to finish by summer's end if he expected to get paid before the new school year started.

"Coralee highly recommended you. It's a deal."

"Okay, then. I'll come by in the morning with some wood samples and we'll go from there."

Chapter 11

The next morning, Emily went for a run, then showered and sat down to finish final revisions on the true-crime book she was writing. Henry, in agreement with Emily's decision to hire Dallas, had already gone to the hospital; Maddy was still asleep. She hoped once school started again, Maddy would be able to get herself up before noon. Mid-morning, Dallas arrived with cabinet samples.

Emily spread the samples out on the kitchen table. She held the promising ones up to the light, squinted, felt the finish. She narrowed it down to two. "I like the light pine, and the walnut. Is one more durable than the other?"

"They're both good choices."

Maddy came into the kitchen in her pajamas, looking puzzled by the samples spread out over the table.

"Maddy, which wood do you like for the new cabinets?"

"Huh?"

"This is Dallas Peterkin. Coralee recommended him to put in new cabinets."

Maddy ran her hands over the two Emily had set apart. "I like this one."

Dallas said, "That's the pine. It will match nicely with the floors and walls."

"Pine it is," said Emily. "When can you start?"

"I'm doing some work over at the inn, but I can come by later this afternoon and start ripping out the old cabinets."

*So much for working on her book.* Emily imagined clearing out all the cabinets and finding a place to store their contents. "Sure. That would be great."

Her phone rang. "Give me a minute. Hi, Jonathan. That's right. The police don't have any eyewitnesses who can place Robby at the picnic. Only the lunch box and the sweatshirt. Circumstantial, right? Okay. Talk to you later."

She led Dallas to the door. "Sorry, that was important."

"Was it about that guy who killed the young girl? Hope they nail that son of a..."

Maddy interjected. "He didn't do it. They have other suspects."

Emily stepped between Dallas and Maddy. "We'll see you this afternoon, right?"

"You got it."

Emily did a little more writing before lunch. Her legs were aching, no longer acclimatized to running after a two-week hiatus. Being a successful true-crime writer came with its deadlines. This was her third book in as many years and she hoped this one, inspired by her ex-boss and the disappearance of her son, would be as big of a hit as the others. Although she had enjoyed teaching the adult writing course at St. Edwards last summer, she'd turned it down this year. Between the trip to Scotland and her current work in progress, not to mention her new responsibilities as the mother of a teenager, she knew she'd made the right decision.

After lunch, she and Maddy packed dishes away in cardboard boxes. Carefully wrapping each item, she was glad she'd held onto the two-weeks-worth of newspapers accumulated while they were away. They'd just about finished, when Jonathan arrived.

"Did you find anything?" asked Maddy, the moment the door opened.

Emily led Jonathan into the living room. "Maddy, he's barely been in town twenty-four hours." Turning to Jonathan, she said, "I hope you found the inn comfortable."

"Absolutely. And I adore the cat café. My girlfriend back home would be in heaven. Coralee told me you started the entire thing, Maddy."

Emily was a little surprised at an eighty-year-old man having a girlfriend, but more power to him. He did have the most beautiful cobalt-colored eyes.

"It was a school project that just sort of grew," said Maddy.

Jonathan pulled his notes out of his brief case. "I found out Carlson was heading toward bankruptcy paying for his wife's medical care."

"Wasn't that a long time ago? Before I was even born. How does that help Robby *now*?"

"It can help us with reasonable doubt. If he had a motive to kill his own wife, the jury just might believe he killed his much younger girlfriend. We can plant the seed, deflecting the sole suspicion off Robby."

"Is that all you've got? Isn't Vermont one of those right-to-die states?"

"Maddy! That's rude."

"It's okay, Mrs. Fox. All I'm saying is that's all we have *now*. We're just getting started."

"Call me Emily. At the post memorial gathering, someone mentioned something about a suicide note on Damari's computer."

"I'll check it out." His phone vibrated on the coffee table. "It's the police station. Yes, Detective O'Leary. I'm the counsel of record, yes. I'll be right down."

"News?" said Emily.

"The detective got an anonymous call to the tip line. The caller claims to have seen Robby Birchfield at the picnic with Damari Cooper the night she was killed.

I'm afraid with this new discovery, there's no doubt we'll be going to trial. I've got to work fast."

After Jonathan left, Emily couldn't concentrate on her book. Maddy was panicked and peppered her with questions she couldn't answer.

"I don't know if they can use an anonymous tip, or if they can trace the call."

"Can't the police interview people who were at the picnic and ask if they saw Professor Carlson there?"

"Again, that's a question for Jonathan, or Detective Megan." She felt her blood pressure rising, just watching Maddy's agitation and being unable to provide answers. She was relieved to see Henry walk through the door.

"Everything okay?" He put his keys down on the hallway table.

"The police received another anonymous tip. Someone claims to have seen Robby and Damari together the night she was killed."

"Anonymous tip? If someone had that information, why would they wait until now to call it in? And why anonymous? Robby's been arrested, it's not like he'd be a threat."

"Maybe that's exactly why they waited. You know this town. Once Robby was arrested, I'm sure the news spread like wildfire." Emily sank into the recliner. "We'll have to wait and see what Jonathan comes up with." She could see Maddy wasn't pleased.

Henry walked into the kitchen. "Whoa, looks like a tornado came through here."

Emily, reminded of the project, followed him. "I choose this wood. Maddy liked it too. If you think it looks like a mess now, wait until Dallas comes back and starts pulling out these old cabinets."

"He isn't wasting any time. I like the wood you chose." He gave her a hug, then turned to his daughter.

"Cheer up, Maddy. I have faith in Robby's legal counsel."

"It's going to be hard to cook in there. We'll have to stock up on paper plates."

"It's a perfect excuse to go to the inn for dinner, right, Maddy?" He and Emily both knew how much seeing the cats cheered up Maddy.

Emily had almost forgotten Dallas Peterkin was coming back in the afternoon. She'd just gone back to packing the kitchen when she heard Henry answer the door.

"How's your wife doing?" asked Henry. "Last time I saw her she was ecstatic there had been no damage to her head or to the baby. Can't believe it's been a whole year already. She was lucky. Most hospitals this size don't have the latest equipment like we do. I was happy I was able to reassure her there were no injuries."

"She and the baby are doing great. It was a girl. Alexandra Sophie."

"Daughters are a blessing." Henry brought Dallas to the kitchen. "So did you bring a wrecking ball or something?"

"Nah. Just the tools in my box and a little muscle."

"Come on, Emily. Put that down and let's let the man work."

It wasn't easy to relax with the cacophony coming from the kitchen, but Emily flipped through the channels. Neither was a regular daytime television watcher. She turned up the volume, distracted by the sound coming from the kitchen.

"So, a TV shrink trying to get a stubborn teen to go to rehab, a show about the wonders of kale and how to make twenty recipes using it, or seeing if the judge awards damages to the lady whose ex deliberately crashed his car through the side of her trailer. This is what we've been missing?" said Henry.

"Want to go for a walk?"

"Yeah, but I don't want to leave Maddy alone here with a stranger."

"Emily, Henry, you have to see this," called Dallas. They ran into the kitchen where Dallas held a cabinet in his hand. He nodded toward the wall. "Take a look. In the wall."

Emily gasped. Henry grabbed a flashlight and said. "What on earth?"

"Take it out," said Emily. She grabbed the flashlight from Henry.

Henry reached in, pulling out a tarnished, silver box that fit in his two cupped hands. "It has a padlock. How are we going to get it open?"

Maddy wandered into the kitchen. "What's that?"

"A silver box, hidden behind the cabinets in the wall," said Henry. He pulled at the lock.

"If you want it open, I can do that," said Dallas. Given the go ahead, he fished in his toolbox for a pair of pliers. Without too much difficulty, he broke the lock open.

Maddy said, "What if it's cursed? Maybe we should leave it closed. Whoever buried it in the wall may have had a good reason."

"You mean like Pandora's box?" said Henry. "Don't be silly." He lifted the creaky lid, with three pair of eyes, in addition to his own, glued to the contents.

Emily lifted out a playing card, several envelopes sealed with wax, imprinted with the letter F, and a skeleton key. "What on earth?"

The envelopes each had a Roman numeral written calligraphy style under the wax seal. Henry held up number one. "Should I open it?"

"Yes!" shouted Emily and Maddy. Dallas nodded.

Henry carefully opened the envelope. "It's some kind of riddle. It says *What has a mouth but cannot speak, runs but has no legs?*

"Is it a joke?" said Maddy. "Who left it there?"

"My grandfather built this place from the ground up. It had to be someone in my family."

Emily said, "It's so bizarre. Who did he expect to find it?"

"My grandfather loved games. He died when I was ten, but I remember he taught me to play Checkers and started teaching me Chess."

"No wonder you love Sudoku so much," said Maddy. "It's genetic."

Emily said, "What are we supposed to do with this? And why the playing card? An ace of spades?"

"I'm more curious about the key," said Maddy.

Dallas said, "Should I continue? Maybe there's buried treasure in there too."

"Go ahead. I think we're going out to dinner later but you can work until then," said Emily.

She couldn't imagine what the odd items added up to. It had to have been put there by Henry's grandfather, right? What kind of a game had he been playing and who was meant to find the silver box? She sat at her desk, trying to write, but her mind kept wandering back and forth from Robby's predicament to this new puzzle. And her legs ached.

Chapter 12

Emily gave up on writing and, instead, stretched out on her bed, popped two Advil, and closed her eyes. Chester curled up beside her, hogging half her pillow. His soothing purr, white noise, lulled her to sleep.

She woke up with a start. Sweating. Heart racing. Maddy—chased by someone whose face she couldn't make out. She ran after them. The attacker sped up. She ran faster—until she collapsed, arms outstretched, never reaching them. She sat up, caught her breath, and looked around the bedroom, anchoring herself. *It was just a bad dream. Maddy is fine.*

She glanced at her phone and turned off the alarm seconds before it had been set to go off. She washed her face, put on a bit of eyeliner and foundation, then pulled on denim capris and a fitted floral shirt.

Henry opened the door. "Are you okay."

Her heart beat had normalized. "I'm fine."

"Ready? We should get going."

They piled into the Jeep. Maddy put on her Dr. Beats, a blindfold for the ears. At the inn, Emily introduced Jonathan to Henry.

"I'm glad you could join us for dinner," said Henry.

"The walk from my room nearly killed me." Jonathan coughed, paused, then broke into a laugh. "I'm kidding. I may look old but I've got the body of a fifty–year-old." He flexed his arm and Emily marveled at the hint of a wrinkled bicep peeking out from the sleeve of his royal blue polo shirt.

Maddy quickly checked on the cats, then joined them at the table. "Coralee has that eggplant and couscous dish on the menu tonight. I saw it on the specials when I came in."

"Maddy and I are vegetarians," explained Emily. "Coralee has been wonderful about trying out meatless recipes since Maddy joined us." She assumed her friend Susan had filled him in on their family background before he came, and it seemed to be the case.

"I've given up red meat myself," said Jonathan. "I live on chicken and fish." He turned toward the door. "Isn't that the detective I spoke to earlier?"

Megan and Pat, holding hands, made their way to the table. Henry said, "Fancy meeting you here."

"We only eat here four or five times a week," said Pat. Noticing Jonathan, he extended his hand. "You must be the lawyer from Atlanta."

"Originally Atlanta, but I moved to Westbrook to be near family. I'm Jonathan Stirling."

Megan said, "Jonathan and I met back at the station earlier."

"Why don't you join us?" said Emily. "There's plenty of room."

He nodded and Megan grabbed a chair from a neighboring table.

"These smell great." Pat grabbed a roll. "How do you like Sugarbury Falls?"

"It's charming from the little I've seen. My girlfriend would love this place. Maybe I'll arrange a fall foliage trip for us after this is all over."

"Mr. Stirling, did you make any headway?" asked Megan.

"Call me Jonathan, please. I went out to the college and spoke to Professor Carlson. He was quite evasive when I asked him about spending time with Damari Cooper. Evasive verging on defensive. He insisted the only time he spent with her was supervising her research or teaching a class. And he insists he never set foot at the Founder's Day celebration."

The waitress jotted down their dinner orders and refilled the water glasses.

"Does he have an alibi?" asked Emily.

Megan answered, "I interviewed him as well. His alibi is about as strong as Robby's. He was home alone. Fell asleep watching television. Woke up and went to bed around 3 a.m."

"What happened to the suicide theory?" asked Emily.

"There was a note on her computer that sounded like it could have been a suicide note. Said something about 'love hurting' and 'moving to a greener place without pain.' I ran it by her best friend, Li Min Wang, and she said it sounded nothing like the way Damari would express herself. And Damari had just dropped off a new dress at the cleaners to be hemmed. It's my experience that suicide victims are all about closure. It didn't make sense."

"And there were the bruises across her abdomen," said Pat. "It wasn't a suicide."

"Then why write the note?" Emily took a sip of water.

Maddy grabbed a roll. "Duh. Maybe she didn't write it. Maybe someone, let's say the murderer, wrote it so it'd look like a suicide and didn't think about the telltale bruises."

"That's a plausible theory," said Jonathan. "Megan, did you check for prints?"

"Of course. We only found Damari's."

"She took her laptop to class, right? The professor had access then. He could have written it and wiped his prints while she was out measuring gardenia leaves or something."

"I'm re-interviewing people who spent most of the day at the picnic. I'll be showing them Carlson's picture. Otherwise, no tie-in to the murder."

"But neither he nor Robby has an alibi so why is Robby the one behind bars?"

"Because of the lunch box and sweatshirt found near the crime scene. And the anonymous tip saying he was there that night."

Maddy said, "Did the sweatshirt you found have a missing drawstring?"

"As a matter of fact it did."

"Someone planted it. I searched his drawers for a red sweatshirt. It was missing."

"Searched his…"

"Enough about the murder," said Emily, quickly changing the subject. "Here comes the food and I'm starving. Henry, tell them about our little discovery."

Henry, realizing they didn't want to reveal that Coralee had let them into Robby's room, said, "Dallas Peterkin was ripping out our old kitchen cabinets and found a silver box in the wall which contains a skeleton key, a playing card, and several envelopes sealed with wax imprinted with the letter F. My grandfather must have hidden it there. We opened the first one and it has a riddle." Henry relayed the riddle.

"A river," said Pat.

Henry was surprised. "That was quick."

"A river has a mouth but doesn't talk and runs with no legs. Maybe there's something at St. John's river you're supposed to find."

"That's a bit vague. St. John's river is miles long. And what's with the card?"

"When do you think the box was hidden?" asked Megan.

"The cabin was built nearly a hundred years ago. The box had to have been sealed into the wall when those original cabinets were put in."

"That was right around the time of the Great Depression."

"Weren't people like hoarding their money back then?" said Maddy.

"If he was hoarding money, why wouldn't he have hidden the money in the box rather than leaving those vague clues?" Emily wiped sauce from her mouth. Mysteries seemed to find her like mosquitos buzzing around porch lights at dusk.

While working on dessert, Dan Fischer came in with a pretty young date. Emily whispered to Megan, "She looks like she's twelve."

"Hey, don't we see enough of each other at work?" said Dan to the group. He hugged the young girl like a hard-won trophy.

"Who's your lady friend?" said Emily.

"This is Elsie. She's a nanny, here for the summer."

The girl, who looked slightly older than Maddy, said with a heavy accent, "It's Elsa. I live in Germany but want to see New England. I applied with agency and they found me this work, I mean job."

"Elsie babysits for the children in the cabin next door to me." Dan put his arm around the fair-skinned, rosy-cheeked, beauty. Emily couldn't fathom what the two of them had in common. Did he just squeeze her boob?

"So is this the lawyer you were telling me about?"

"Yeah. Dan, this is Jonathan Stirling. Jonathan, Dan."

Dan said, "That poor kid's going to need a lot of help getting out of this one. Do you have a defense lined up?"

Jonathan sipped his coffee. "We're working on it."

"I heard they found his sweatshirt on the bike path. You know, I saw him and Damari together earlier that day. He was eating a hotdog."

"I'll put the pieces together and, rest assured, Robby Birchfield will have the best defense possible."

The hostess, who'd been waiting patiently, started walking toward a table, menus in hand.

"That's our cue. See you at the hospital, Henry. Enjoy your evening." Elsa waved a shy goodbye as they followed the waitress.

"That's disgusting," said Maddy. "That girl is young enough to be his daughter."

Emily agreed, happy to know Maddy found the age difference to be inappropriate.

"Does the whole town know all the details of the case?" asked Jonathan.

"It's a small town and people talk," said Emily.

A scream. From the far corner of the room. Li Min standing, cursing at Dan.

"You quack! You said we'd have our baby. We paid you. You promised!" Li Min picked up a glass of something and threw it at Dan. "No wonder Damari dumped you."

Shen put his arms on his wife's shoulders and calmly but firmly said, "You'll pay for this Doctor Fischer. That was our life's savings, and you've broken my wife's heart."

Dan wiped his face with the cloth napkin and blotted at his shirt. "There are no guarantees. I told you your uterus was incompetent."

The comment was like throwing oil on the fire of Li Min's anger. "Damari was right about you. She figured you out pretty quickly."

Shen grabbed his wife's wrist as she was about to crack a plate over Dan's head. "Come on, let's get out of here. He's not worth going to jail over."

Shen led his wife out of the dining room, clutching her hand as they made their way past staring diners. Now, Li Min was sobbing as they passed Emily and Henry's table. Elsa, the German nanny, slapped Dan across the face after he whispered something in her ear. Emily could only imagine what insensitive comment he'd made. Elsa stormed out after Li Min and Shen.

Jonathan said, "I misread this as a quiet little town."

Emily said, "That was so strange. I saw Li Min earlier today and she was all smiles—convinced she was pregnant. I didn't know the hospital had an infertility clinic."

"We don't," said Henry. "Anyone with serious infertility issues is referred to the program in Burlington. It's top notch. I can't imagine why they didn't go there."

Maddy said, "What did she mean saying Damari was right about him? Were they dating?"

"No, just colleagues as far as I knew. Megan, did Dan say he and Damari were friends?"

"Just that he knew her as the receptionist in the emergency room. Li Min didn't bring up any relationship between the two when I interviewed her. I'm not sure what the comment meant, if anything."

Maddy said to Megan, "Maybe instead of making a case against Robby, you should look more closely at that Dr. Fischer. He seems to like them young *and* he has gray hair."

Chapter 13

Maddy carried her laptop into the kitchen the next morning while Emily and Henry ate breakfast. Henry was engrossed in his Sudoku, and Emily tore out coupons from the paper.

"There's fresh oatmeal on the stove."

Maddy seemed not to have heard Emily, launching into her news.

"Look, there's another post from that girl. She says she's going to end it all and can't take it anymore. We can't let that happen."

"Megan said they can't trace the post. She hasn't made a threat to society or committed a crime. It's really tragic, but I don't know what to do. Did you suggest counseling?"

Maddy gave her a look. "Counseling? What, on-line? Or maybe she could skype with Dr. Phil."

"You don't have to be sarcastic. I'm trying to think of something."

Henry said, "There's a suicide hotline at the hospital. Why don't you post the number?"

"I'm going to private message her and see if she answers." She typed a message, then ladled oatmeal into a Styrofoam bowl.

"I don't know why you bought these. You know they'll wind up in a landfill."

Emily was tired of the endless criticisms. "It's just while the kitchen is being remodeled."

"What about following up on that Dr. Fischer?"

Henry said, "I'll stop by and have a talk with Dan when I get to the hospital."

"He's not going to tell you the truth if he was seeing Damari. Even if he didn't kill her, why would he admit to having a relationship and make himself a suspect?"

Emily, admiring Maddy's pragmatism, grabbed a glass of juice. "I have a better idea. We can stop by Rebecca and Abby's place. Rebecca is a whiz at this sort of thing. She might find a connection between the two of them."

Maddy said, "While we're at it, how about the infertility business that Li Min was so upset about. I think there's more to that story."

"I was going to ask him about that when I see him." Henry looked at the rooster clock. "As a matter of fact, I need to get going. I'll talk to him first thing."

Henry grabbed his briefcase and kissed Emily good-bye. On the way to the hospital, he sorted out what he knew about Dan Fischer. Dan was about his age and had been an ob-gyn back in California before coming to Vermont. He mentioned an ex-wife once, but never talked about her. As far as he knew, he didn't have children. He was a bit of a charmer. When he thought about it, Dan didn't hesitate to give hugs or kiss his patients on the cheek. Was he acting fatherly, or was it something else?

He jumped out of the Jeep at the same time Pat pulled into the parking lot.

"Hey, buddy. That was quite a scene last night. Megan says she's going to look into the whole connection between Damari and Dan."

"She thinks what Li Min said is valid?"

"Not really. She thinks Li Min probably just blurted out the comment about Damari in anger, but they have to follow up on it."

"Have you noticed how Dan always puts his arm around the nurses when he talks to them?"

"I think it's just his personality."

"I didn't know he was some kind of infertility guru, did you?"

"No, but down in the morgue, I'm not as privy to that sort of info as those upstairs. Wait. This is probably nothing, but…"

"Spit it out. What?"

"Right after Christmas I did an autopsy on a young girl who died from an overdose of infertility hormones. The husband said she never sought help from an infertility clinic."

"Did the records say she was Dan Fischer's patient?"

"No. Her primary care doctor was all that was listed, and her husband confirmed she didn't have an ob-gyn. He was rather tight-lipped about the whole thing which I thought at the time seemed strange."

"Did you call in the police?"

"No. I had no reason to think a crime had been committed. Figured she misjudged the dosage—or her husband did when he went to give her a shot. In the back of my mind, I thought that's why the husband seemed weird. Anyhow, I went off on vacation right after that and didn't give it another thought."

"Can you access her medical records?"

Pat punched a few keys on his computer. "Give me a minute." He clicked more keys. "This is strange. I can't find her records."

"Do you have the name right?"

"Yeah. Her name was Sunshine Blue. I remember thinking it sounding like something Beyoncé would name her kid. Look, I still have it in my rolodex."

"Rolodex?"

"What can I say. I'm an old-fashioned kind of guy. It's handier than going through medical records for contact info on the rare occasions I need it." He pulled out the card. "See."

Henry looked at the card, then sat at the computer. "Let me try." He tried alternate spellings, but still nothing.

"You couldn't find it either, right?"

"It's not even been a year. I'm sure the records should still be on file. Maybe we can check with her primary care doctor. Do you know who it was?"

"No, but there are only two in this town. We can ask them."

Pat locked his door and they rode the elevator to the main floor. One of the two doctors was on duty. He was sitting behind the desk doing paperwork.

"Jack, do you have a minute?" asked Henry.

"What's up Henry? Pat, why are you up here? I swear I didn't kill anybody lately."

Henry said, "We had some questions about a patient and Pat says she only listed a primary care doctor."

"I can't remember which of the two of you she listed. Do you remember a patient named Sunshine Blue?" Pat half-sat on the desk as he spoke.

"No. I would have remembered a name like that. Why don't you look up her records?"

"They seem to have disappeared," said Pat.

"Can't you call her and ask?"

"No, she died last winter. I did the autopsy."

"Sorry I can't help. I'd have remembered a patient who died. Doesn't happen every day you know."

Henry and Pat thanked the doctor, and went to Henry's office. According to one of the nurses, the other primary care doctor, Dr. Madison Pollack, had an office in town, Henry picked up the phone.

"Hello, this is Dr. Henry Fox. I need to speak with Dr. Pollack, ugh, regarding a case." He waited while the receptionist got her. "Dr. Pollack, do you remember a patient named Sunshine Blue?" He cupped the receiver and whispered to Pat, "She doesn't think so, but she's checking the computer." A few minutes later, she was back on the line. "You didn't? Thank you for your time."

"I take it that was a no," said Pat.

"Yeah. She even checked the records. She said sometimes she'll only see a patient once and they list her as their doctor. That wasn't the case this time."

"Should we ask Doctor Dan about her?"

"I'm not sure that's the route to take. If he is running some sort of sketchy infertility clinic, let's not tip him off."

"You want to call Megan?"

"Not until we investigate a bit ourselves. I don't want her to think we're pulling things out of thin air. I wonder if we can get a look at Dr. Dan's files."

"You think he'd be dumb enough to have kept them?"

"They aren't in the system, but if he's treating infertility, he has to be keeping records on his patients somewhere." Pat was silent for several minutes. Henry knew he was formulating a plan. "How about you distract him. Get him out of his office quickly, so he doesn't lock up, and I'll sneak in and search."

"We can give it a shot, but I can't believe he'd leave those sorts of records easily accessible."

After discussing a plan, Pat hid against the wall around the corner from Dan's office, while Henry went inside.

"Dan, come quick. There's a woman in the ER in labor big time. I think the baby's coming any minute now! Come on." Henry and Dan ran down the hall to the elevator. When the elevator bell rang, Pat snuck into the office. He searched through the files in Dan's bottom drawer, and then the filing cabinet. Flipping through the first two drawers, he found dusty files packed tightly together. They were coded according to hospital protocol. The third drawer, however, was locked. He tried to jimmy it, to no avail, kicked it, then snuck back out before Henry returned with Dan.

"Henry, she couldn't have gone far. You sure she was that close to giving birth? Why would she have left, that's crazy."

"I don't know. She was upset and screaming. Her husband was with her. Maybe when I went to fetch you, they got fed up and went elsewhere. Seemed imminent, but then again, I haven't delivered a baby since med school."

"Like where would they go? There's not another hospital for miles. Maybe we should call the police. If you're right, she's probably having that baby on the side of the road somewhere."

Like divine intervention, the loudspeaker echoed in the hall. "Dr. Fischer, you're needed in labor and delivery, stat."

"I've gotta go. I'd follow up if I were you."

After Dan took off down the hall, Pat grabbed Henry's arm. "There's a locked drawer in his filing cabinet. I'll bet he's got records in there."

"Then it's time to tell your girlfriend to get a search warrant."

"I'm sure my hunch isn't enough for a warrant, but I'll tell her what we learned. See you later, Sherlock."

Chapter 14

While Henry was at the hospital, Emily and Maddy walked over to Rebecca and Abby's place. Abby was photographing flowers in their garden and smiled as soon as she saw them. "Come on in. Rebecca's making bread."

Emily's stomach growled when she drank in the aroma of freshly baked bread the minute she walked through the door. Rebecca dusted off her hands and offered them drinks. "What can I help you with?"

Emily was embarrassed. "I'm sorry. It seems every time I come by it's to get technical help."

"Don't be silly. I enjoy it."

Abby walked into the living room with a basket of bread. "Here, have some."

Emily took a bite. She'd put on ten pounds since moving to Sugarbury Falls, even with her running. "This is delicious. You could start a business."

"Just a hobby. My photography business keeps me plenty busy."

Emily turned to Rebecca. "Can you dig up some information on Dr. Dan Fischer? He lived in California before coming here. See if there were any complaints filed."

"Sure, I can search. By the way, I got some more info on Professor Carlson. No charges were ever filed in his wife's death because he had an alibi. One he didn't want made public."

"An affair?"

"An AA meeting. He didn't want it made public, but enough members came forward despite anonymity to vouch for the fact he was there all evening."

"Then who gave his wife all that morphine?"

"She wasn't yet all that incapacitated. Her prints were found on the morphine bottle. Consensus was she did it herself. Carlson tried to keep that under wraps too. Didn't want her memory tainted."

"So he had a heart. Wasn't a demon after all. That'll make it harder to cast suspicion on him in court."

"There's more. I dug far and wide and couldn't find any evidence that he did anything more than advise Damari or any past students. He had a history of mentoring students and including them in on his research. I don't think he's your guy."

Emily sipped her lemonade, while Maddy scratched Milo between the ears. With Carlson looking doubtful, Emily was now convinced the gray-haired man was actually Dan Fischer. Fischer claimed he saw Damari at the picnic, but not at the fireworks later that evening. Was he at the festivities continually, or did he slip out to meet Damari? She looked at Rebecca, who seemed to have found something.

"Emily, this is interesting. Your Dr. Dan received frequent packages from a pharmaceutical lab in Mexico City. Doesn't he use the pharmacy at the hospital?"

"You hacked into the postal service?" Maddy sounded impressed. Emily made a note to discuss this with her later.

"It's all in a day's work," said Rebecca. "How does that tie into him as Damari's killer?"

"I'm not sure. Maybe she found out what he was up to and threatened to turn him in. She worked at the hospital. It's not out of reach to think she heard things."

Maddy tossed Milo a toy. "Or she was an egg donor."

"What?" Both Rebecca and Emily stared at her.

"As long as we're brainstorming…"

"She could be right," said Rebecca.

Emily's phone vibrated. "It's Jonathan, Robby's lawyer. He says he has some new information and we should meet him at Coralee's."

"Hope it works in Robby's favor."

"Thanks, Rebecca. For everything. And Abby, thanks for the bread."

Emily and Maddy walked back to their cabin, to find Dallas, toolbox in hand, waiting on the stoop. Emily had forgotten he was coming.

"Did you open the other envelopes?" said Dallas.

With all the events since yesterday, she'd practically forgotten about the mystery.

"Not yet. Hey, would you mind if I let you in, then go out for a bit?"

"I'm trustworthy. I'll lock up when I'm done if you're not back."

"Great. I can't wait to see those new cabinets."

After unlocking the door and flicking on the lights, Emily and Maddy jumped in the Audi. Jonathan's text sounded urgent, yet optimistic. He had gone to interview witnesses from the picnic. Maybe he'd found someone who saw Damari with Dan Fischer, or came up with some sort of alibi for Robby. Emily turned on the wipers, imagining the drops of rain were Mrs. Cooper's tears. Did love for your biological child keep growing over time, or was your heart saturated with love the first time you held your baby? Her love for Maddy was more like the way she fell in love with Henry. It started slowly, grew, then overcame her.

"What do you think those clues mean?" said Maddy. "We didn't even get a chance to open the others."

"We can do it tonight when Henry's home. Don't get your hopes up. It might be from an old Easter egg hunt for all we know."

She pulled into the parking lot, noticing the rain had kept visitors off the usually teeming front porch. "Come on, Maddy. Let's go right to his room. You can visit the cats later."

Jonathan opened the door. The walls were bright yellow, with an accent wall covered in green and white striped wallpaper. An ivory duvet covered the four poster bed.

"Not a whole lot of sitting room, but you're welcome to the desk chair, Emily."

Maddy sat on the edge of the bed. "Did you find something to clear Robby?"

"I found a witness who saw Damari with an older man out on the lake, must have been just before she died. He was out fishing and saw an older gentleman stand up in the boat. The man appeared to be angry because he was stomping and the boat shook side to side."

"Why didn't he get help?" said Maddy.

"He was with his grandson and wanted to shield him from it."

Emily said, "Can he identify the man as Carlson?"

"No, but here's the thing. The detectives have CCTV footage of Carlson getting gas near his home at dusk, the same time the witness saw the boat. Carlson was clear across town. He couldn't have been two places at once."

"And what's the likelihood that Damari was with two different gray-haired men on the same night, in a boat." Emily wondered if the witness could identify the man in the boat as Dr. Dan Fischer. "If we showed him a picture, do you think he would recognize the man in the boat?"

"You're thinking it was that doctor I met at dinner the other night. The man gave me a description, though he wasn't close enough to clearly see the face. He said the man was wearing a light-weight navy jacket with a hood—like a rain jacket. I checked the footage of Professor Carlson. He had on a tan, wool jacket when he was pumping gas."

"Did you tell the police?"

"Of course. Detective O'Leary and I spent quite some time together going over the evidence after I found that witness."

Maddy said, "We ruled out Carlson, and a witness saw Damari with an older man in the boat. Isn't that enough to clear Robby?"

"Detective O'Leary and her partner are picking up the witness as we speak. Hopefully, it's enough for reasonable doubt, but if we can prove Robby was nowhere near the lake that night we'd have a strong defense. I have to get back to work."

"Call us if you find anything new," said Emily.

"Emily, can't we stop and see the cats?"

"Of course."

They opened the door to the cat café and carefully made their way in. Coralee's son, Noah, had built a second door so the cats couldn't escape. The instructions outside the café said to close the first door before opening the second glass door.

Half a dozen cats were in full view, while others hid inside cat tents and behind furniture. A gray tabby and a calico were perched on the cat tree Henry made for them. Two black cats, one twice the size of the other, slept in cat beds on the floor. A white cat, who Maddy had named Annie, slept in a large tube in front of the wall with the jungle mural.

Maddy picked up a feather cat toy and coaxed the larger black cat into playing. A young couple sat on a sofa petting a sandy colored cat with long hair.

The woman said, "Excuse me, but do you know the process for adopting a cat?"

"Sure. There are applications right here." She handed the young lady a clipboard. "Are you going to adopt?"

"We've been visiting this little lady for weeks, and have decided we can't wait to make her part of our family. Meet LuLu." She scooped up the cat and nuzzled it.

"Congratulations! She had a sister who was adopted a while ago."

The young man stood up. "Whoever came up with the idea for this place was a genius. In a million years I never would have figured out I was a cat person if I hadn't started tagging along with my wife."

Emily burst with pride over what Maddy had accomplished. To think the cat café idea was born because of Sugarbury High's community service graduation requirement!

After their quick stop at the cat café, she and Maddy headed home. She'd forgotten that she'd left Dallas to work on the kitchen and was startled for a moment when she saw a van in her driveway. She joked about becoming senile when she forgot where she'd put her reading glasses or whether or not she'd started the dishwasher, but in the back of her mind, she worried if it was true. She just didn't feel as sharp or quick as she did in her forties.

When they walked into the cabin, Dallas was packing his toolbox. Emily looked around the kitchen, which looked like it had suffered the wrath of a determined tornado. She tried to smile, and said, "It's really coming along."

"Yeah," said Dallas. "Getting rid of the old cabinets is half the battle right there. Do you want me to stack them outside?"

Emily hadn't even thought about it and decided to talk to Henry first. Maybe he could use some of the scraps in one of his woodworking projects. "Not yet."

"I heard something on the news about that girl who was killed. They caught the guy, right? Said they were preparing for a trial."

"It's not a slam dunk. We were just talking to the young man's lawyer and there are other suspects the police are considering."

"Really? I heard he was seen with her the night of the murder and that they found his shirt or something at the crime scene. Not a slam dunk?"

"Innocent until proven guilty," said Emily. "Things aren't always as they seem. Shouldn't you be getting home to that wife and baby of yours?"

Dallas looked at his watch. "I didn't realize it was that late. I'll try to come back tomorrow after I finish up at the inn."

As Dallas started his van, Henry pulled into the driveway. Chester heard the Jeep and jumped down from the back of the sofa to wait in front of the cabin door. Henry came in bearing a large pizza box.

"You read my mind," said Emily. "I was wondering how I was going to maneuver in that kitchen. Dallas tore out the old cabinets and I didn't know if you wanted to save any of the wood."

"I think the remnants of the kitchen before have seen their day and deserve to rest in peace at the town dump. Did you see Jonathan?"

"Yes, and he found something interesting. A witness who was fishing with his grandson came forward and said he saw a gray-haired man in the boat with Damari the night she died."

"That professor, Carlson, right?"

"No. The police have Carlton on CCTV at the time the witness saw the man in the boat. He's a dead end. We're looking for yet another gray-haired man."

Maddy said, "I told you to look at that doctor who Li Min was yelling at. Dr. Fischer, right?"

"I'm beginning to think so," said Henry. "Pat said a woman died of an overdose of an infertility drug about six months ago. When we tried to find the records, they didn't exist."

"And she was Dan Fischer's patient?" asked Emily.

"Bingo. And that's not all."

Maddy scooped up Chester. "Well, tell us."

"Dan was receiving packages from a pharmaceutical company in Mexico. We have a pharmacy at the hospital. He'd have no reason to be importing drugs."

"Unless he had a side business helping infertile couples, right? Did you explore the idea that Damari was an egg donor?"

"Maddy, that's creative, but there's no evidence of it."

Emily said, "We could talk to Li Min. She was Damari's best friend. Maybe she was donating eggs for Li Min!"

"I'll pass the idea along to the detectives," said Henry.

"Can't we just talk to her first? The whole idea sounds far-fetched. It'd be better if we had something more concrete to go to them with."

Changing the subject, Henry said, "We never opened the other envelopes! Let's eat our pizza out here in the living room and see if we can figure out what Grandpa was trying to tell us."

Emily grabbed paper plates and napkins from the kitchen and set them on the coffee table, while Chester surreptitiously lifted his paws onto the pizza box. Henry shooed him away.

"Okay, so the first envelope gave us a clue about a river. Maddy, open up the next one," said Henry.

She carefully opened the yellowed envelope with the number *two*. "In the chiming comes unity as many tones turn into one."

"Huh?" said Henry.

"What chiming places do we know of around here?" said Emily.

"There's that hand bell choir that plays in the amphitheater."

"And doorbells sound like chimes," added Emily. "Was there ever a doorbell here at the cabin?"

"Not that I remember," said Henry. "Open number three."

Maddy peeled off the wax seal and carefully removed the next clue. "The curfew tolls the knell of parting day; there at the foot of yonder nodding Beech that wreathes its old fantastic roots so high, his listless length at noontide would he stretch and pour upon the brook that babbles by."

"That sounds familiar," said Henry.

"It's from a poem. Maddy, grab my laptop." Emily typed in a quick search. "Here it is. *Elegy on a Country Churchyard* by Thomas Gray." She skimmed the poem. "Here! The lines are right out of this poem."

Henry's phone vibrated. "It's the hospital." He took the phone into the kitchen.

"Maddy, the clues are from the poem. Let's see what we have so far."

"Obviously, it points to a cemetery. Maybe there's buried treasure there."

"What about the Beech and the babbling brook? That has to mean something."

"So we have a river, chimes, and a cemetery," said Maddy. She carefully tore open the fourth envelope.

"Well?" said Emily, looking over Maddy's shoulder.

"I don't know what this is. Looks like a code or maybe an anagram. *ragdemtill*. What's that mean?"

Henry ran back into the living room. "I've got to go. There was a hit and run in front of the hospital. I'll call when I can." He took his plate of pizza and ran out the door.

Chapter 15

Henry rushed into the emergency room. "What have we got?"

"It's one of our own. Chauncey Wells."

"The nurse?"

"Yeah. He was struck by a car crossing the parking lot. A witness said a car screeched by out of nowhere and didn't stop even for a moment."

"A hit and run." Henry ran to the cubicle, where an intern stood over the husky, black body covered with road rash. Henry carefully examined the body. "Looks like several broken bones. Get me the portable ultrasound, and bolus two liters of normal saline. His pressure is low."

Henry ran the ultrasound over his patient. "There's fluid in the abdomen. Positive fast exam."

One of the nurses entered Henry's notes on her iPad and said, "Witnesses say it was intentional."

A few years ago, Henry would have fluffed off the comment, but after his experiences in Sugarbury Falls, he gave it serious consideration.

"His wife should be here any minute." The nurse adjusted his IV.

"When she gets here, have the consent forms ready. Order a CT scan and prep him for surgery. On second thought, let's get him right up to the OR. I'll contact the surgeon on call."

"Detective Wooster is outside. He wants to know if he can interview the victim."

"Certainly not while he's unconscious. I'll speak to him."

Henry found Detective Wooster in the corridor.

"How's he doing?"

"He's in bad shape. Rumors say it was a hit and run."

Detective Wooster said, "There were no skid marks and according to witnesses, the car made no attempt to stop."

"So it was deliberate?"

"We're at the early stages of assessment. When can I speak to the victim?"

"He's going to surgery. It'll be at least a few hours and I can't guarantee he'll be conscious."

"What can you tell me about him?" Detective Wooster pulled out a tablet.

"He's been an ER nurse since I started here. He's well liked, especially since his family owns the barbecue place downtown and he shows up bearing ribs at least once a week. The other nurses can probably tell you more."

Henry went back in to check on Chauncey one last time. Damari and Chauncey both worked here in the ER. Was there some connection between the two incidents? Did it have something to do with imported pharmaceuticals or fertility treatments? Had they seen something they weren't supposed to see?

As if on cue, "Paging Dr. Fischer. Dr. Fischer to ER," boomed through the PA system. Henry waited in the hallway. The announcement was repeated. Again, Henry waited to see if Dan would show up. When he didn't, Henry went up to Dan's office. The door was open and the light on.

"Dan, are you here?" He felt the mug of coffee on the desk, which was still warm. Maybe he went to the restroom, or he finally heard the page. He walked behind the desk and noticed the open drawer in the filing cabinet next to the desk. He flipped through. The files were alphabetized, but those between the letters of *m* and *q* were missing. He went out into the hall, then knocked on the bathroom door.

"Dan, are you in there? Dan, it's Henry."

When he got no response, he went back down to the ER and asked the nurses if they'd seen him.

"No, he never answered the page."

He ran up to Detective Wooster, who was still in the waiting area.

"Do you know what kind of car it was that hit him?"

"The witnesses say it was a white sedan...or a minivan...or an SUV. It sped by so fast, no one caught the make or model."

Henry flew out into the parking lot. Dan drove a white Infinity. He ran to the doctor's area of the parking lot and down the length of cars to Dan's empty spot. Gone. Just like those files. He ran back to the hospital, too late to catch Detective Wooster. He headed back to the parking lot, his Fitbit dinging that he'd met his 10,000 steps for the day.

Driving home, about to call the police, a call came through the Bluetooth.

"Henry, I have to tell you something."

"Dan! Dan, where are you? The police are going to be looking for you. Why did you do it? If you turn yourself in, it'll be better, trust me."

"Turn myself in? You think I killed Damari and ran over that nurse? Some friend."

"Seriously, I'm not judging you."

"Henry, I didn't kill Damari but I know who did. I have proof. Meet me at the diner by the new Walmart. I'm in danger and so are you. The killer's coming after us both. Hurry, and make sure you're not followed."

The phone went dead. On one hand, Henry wanted to turn around and go to the police. On the other, something in Dan's voice made him believe he was telling the truth. He sounded frightened. What if he was right and someone was coming after him next? At the fork in the road, Henry veered right, in the direction of Walmart.

Stepping on the gas, Henry hugged the winding road up the mountain. Dusk had given way to nightfall and it was drizzling, making the glare off the road sting his eyes as it was reflected by the high beams. The road was nearly deserted. He pulled around a turn and came to a screeching stop. The guardrail had given way and fire lit the night sky off past the mountain's edge. He ran out of the car and looked over the side. His stomach churned. Down below, a car was blazing. Henry smelled the gasoline scented smoke as it blustered past where he was standing. Taking a few steps closer to the edge of the cliff, his heart dropped. The car on fire was a white Infinity.

Chapter 16

"Henry, are you okay?" asked Emily. She'd made him a cup of tea and wrapped an afghan around his shoulders.

"I can't believe he's dead. I don't get it."

"The police are sure it wasn't an accident?"

"They're sure. They saw skid marks in the mud by the side of the road. They think he was run down by some sort of truck."

"Just when we were convinced Dan was responsible for Damari's murder. Do you think it was one of his fertility patients? Maybe Li Min or her husband."

"Those two drive a little Smart Car. I saw them get out of it at Coralee's. There's a connection here that we're missing. First Damari, then Chauncey, and now..." He wasn't sure he should tell Emily what Dan said to him before he died.

"You're hiding something. Tell me what it is?"

Maddy came in holding a sandwich. "Henry, eat something."

He was touched by the gesture and took a bite. Chester jumped up on the couch, lured by the smell of ham.

"Henry," said Emily, "What are you hiding?"

"I spoke to Dan on the phone in the car. He said someone was after him and to watch out because I was going to be next."

Maddy's face turned pale. He didn't want to worry her like that. She was super sensitive about losing loved ones since her mother's death. He wished Emily would have laid off until he could have told her in private.

"How do you know he was telling the truth? He could have been trying to get attention off himself. After all, he was suspected of killing Damari. We still don't know he didn't."

"He said he had proof. So much for that. Nothing survived in that car fire."

"Are you sure? Did the police tell you that?"

"Emily, lay off. Whatever proof he had is gone, and by the tone of his voice, I'm convinced he was scared, and that he didn't kill Damari."

Maddy said, "Does this clear Robby? He's in jail. He couldn't have gone after that nurse or Dr. Fischer."

"I don't know. It's all a jumble in my head right now. I know that some files were missing out of Dan's office, the *n, o,* and *p* files. And it looked like he'd left in a hurry." He poked at the fire Emily had started in the fireplace.

"You should finish your sandwich and get some rest."

"Sounds good to me. I'm exhausted." He tore off the crust, finished what was left of his ham sandwich, and kissed Emily goodnight. Then he climbed the ladder to the loft bedroom. He fell asleep as soon as his head hit the fluffy pillow.

Emily and Maddy ate leftover quiche in front of the crackling fire. Dan told Henry that someone was going to come after him. Was that meant to throw him off track, or was it true? What if someone blew up Henry's car next? She just wanted Damari's killer found and this whole thing to be over. Maybe they'd prove Dan killed her and that would be that. When they finished, Rebecca came by. Emily explained in a nutshell the events of the evening.

"Poor Henry," said Rebecca. "Imagine seeing your friend burn up like that."

Maddy shuddered. Emily put the afghan she'd given to Henry over her daughter's shoulders and gave Rebecca a stern look.

"I'm sorry. That was really blunt. I found out about your Dr. Fischer, but now…"

"What?" said Emily.

"I don't like speaking poorly of the dead."

Emily sat at the edge of the sofa. "If you have anything that can help us make sense of this, just say it."

"Did you prove Robby's innocent?" said Maddy.

"Fischer wrote a generous check to the husband of that woman who died from the hormone overdose. No wonder he didn't sue the good doctor."

"Can you connect Damari to the fertility business?" said Emily.

"Nope. No evidence that Dr. Fischer was hiring egg donors or surrogates. Just importing those drugs from Mexico, which isn't exactly illegal."

"Ill regulated and cheaper, right?" said Emily.

"And untraceable. Or they were supposed to be," added Maddy.

Emily said, "Then it has to be that Damari knew or saw something that incriminated him. Surely Li Min told her she was working with the doctor. She made no attempt to hide it."

"But did she know about the imported drugs? And did she find evidence of him harming his fertility patients? I'll keep digging," said Rebecca.

"Where are my manners? We have coffee left from dinner. I'll get us some." She gave the fire a poke before heading to the kitchen.

"Maddy, did you hear any more from that girl on Facebook?" said Rebecca.

"I sent her the number for the suicide hotline. She never answered back. I did some research. Did you know that after accidents, suicide is the leading cause of death in young adults 15-24?"

"I had no idea. I would have thought drugs or alcohol."

"I read that more than 5,000 teens a day attempt suicide, and 1 in 5 seriously consider it."

"I believe it. I came out as gay when I was in high school. Social media hadn't yet taken off, but the comments and the disapproval from my classmates and even friends of my parents were unbearable. I considered suicide myself."

"That's awful!" said Maddy. "What got you through it?"

"My parents were really supportive, and I made friends with a boy in my class who was also gay. That helped a lot. Do you know why she's considering suicide?"

"Not really. Just that she feels alone."

"I followed up after you asked me for help," said Rebecca. "You can report this directly to Facebook. On the post, go to the pull down arrow. You can choose to message her directly, which you already did, or you can report the post to Facebook anonymously. They will message your friend saying someone is concerned about them and they can link her directly to the suicide prevention lifeline."

"I don't want her to think I snitched on her," said Maddy.

Emily, who'd been listening as she retrieved the coffee, said, "They won't say her name, right, Rebecca?"

"They won't. Besides, even if she knows it's you that reported it, wouldn't it make her feel like someone cares?" She looked at her watch. "I'd better get going. I told Abby I'd just be a few minutes and I don't want her to worry."

Emily locked the door behind her, checking three more times that it was indeed secure. She flashed back to when Maddy herself tried to overdose in foster care after her mother's death. That's what prompted Henry and her to fly to Chicago and step up as guardians. She assumed that was why Maddy had taken such an interest in this girl. Thank God Maddy didn't succeed.

"Emily, I'm going to bed," said Maddy. She scooped up Chester from the back of the sofa.

"Goodnight, honey."

"Maybe tomorrow Robby will finally come home."

She wished it was that simple. There were two ways to approach this. First, they could prove Dan was the murderer. The detectives may go through his things and find some sort of proof that he killed Damari. The motive? To keep her from divulging information about his fertility business. Or, they were lovers and had a big fallout. It wouldn't have been good for his reputation if they found he was dating a colleague half his age. But then, who killed Dan?

If Dan is innocent, it's likely the same person who killed Damari killed him, and was now after Henry. A chill ran through her body. And what about the hit and run in front of the hospital? She doubted that was a coincidence. What was the common bond between the four of them?

And there was a third possibility. Robby found out Damari was involved with Dan and killed her out of jealousy. For Maddy's sake, she prayed that wasn't the reason.

Chapter 17

Henry woke feeling rested and it took a minute before he remembered the sight of Dan's car burning up off the side of the road. He could still smell the fire. Dan had been his colleague ever since he and Emily moved to Sugarbury Falls. He was beginning to consider him a friend since the golf outing and more frequent meet ups in the hospital cafeteria. What if Dan was telling the truth? What if someone *was* coming after him next? He didn't want to say much in front of Emily and Maddy, but he couldn't deny worrying about their safety. Emily's came into the room and kicked off her running shoes.

"Hey, did you have a good run?"

"I did. I ran into Kurt and Prancer. He went on about how nice of a kid Robby is and how he hated to think of him in jail."

"After meeting him, I tend to agree. Besides, Maddy is a good judge of character and she thinks he's innocent." Seeing Emily damp from her run, not to mention smelling the efforts of her workout, inspired him to strap on his Fitbit.

"I'm going to shower. The coffee's made."

"Thanks. I'm going to leave a few minutes early and check in on Chauncey."

Henry left for the hospital, pulling the door behind him to make sure it was secure. He didn't know much about Dan's family, just that he'd been married a few times, and hoped the police could find who to notify about his death. It was hard to stop replaying the scene from last night—the bent guardrail, getting out of his car, smelling smoke, Dan's car on fire... In his gut, he felt Dan was innocent, and the warning he gave him about being next was intense and reeked of sincerity.

When he arrived at the hospital, he went directly to Chauncey's room.

"There hasn't been any change," said the nurse. "We still have him listed as critical."

Henry looked at Chauncey's bruised face with the swollen eyelids. Although he'd been a doctor for thirty years, he'd never hardened to the sight of injured patients. His empathy was one of the reasons he chose radiology over emergency medicine. True, he worked here in the ER, but normally the worst he encountered in Sugarbury Falls was someone needing a few stitches or perhaps a broken bone.

A pretty black woman came into the room with a small suitcase and a Styrofoam cup. "I brought him some clothes and his favorite CDs. Chauncey's a big baby when he's sick. Wait till he wakes up and looks in the mirror. All these wires and tubes. I can barely find a spot to touch him."

"You must be Chauncey's wife. I'm so sorry this happened."

"The police asked me if he had any enemies. *Why would they ask that?* you say. They think someone did this on purpose. That's why. I say to them *Chauncey ain't got no enemies. The man would give you the shirt off his back.*"

"I know. We've worked together for some time. He's wonderful with the patients."

"What's with all the beeping and flashing? Does he really need all these machines?"

"For the moment, yes."

"I saw you here last night. He's gonna be okay, right?"

Henry hated being asked that question. "He's a fighter and he's in the best hands. Those nurses are his friends and, believe me, he'll get the royal treatment." Little did she know how badly his liver had been lacerated or that they had to remove his spleen.

The wife pulled out a CD and portable CD player which she busily set out to get working. She found an outlet behind the bedside table.

"I'll stop by later. Let me or the nurses know if you need anything." He closed the door behind him and took the elevator down to the morgue. He imagined how he'd feel if it was Emily unconscious in that hospital bed with the bandages and wires and a chill ran through him. He opened the door to the morgue.

"Hey, buddy. You doing okay? I heard what happened last night."

"I was sure Megan would fill you in."

"She mentioned it was no accident. Who had it in for Dan? I mean, he was a bit of a player, but to be angry enough to kill him?"

"It may not have been out of anger, but out of fear. I'm thinking Dan knew something the killer didn't want revealed."

"Like what? His affair with Damari."

"How do you know he was…"

"The rumor mill. Heck, even being isolated down here I heard it. Didn't pay much attention to it, but now."

"Now what?"

"It makes sense her ex-boyfriend wanted to get even."

"He's sitting in a jail cell. Besides, you're not making sense. I think whoever killed Damari also killed Dan. It's too unlikely that we have more than one murderer running around Sugarbury Falls." He cleared his throat, thinking back to Kurt's tenant and that dead biker last summer. "At least not at the same time."

"What about the whole fertility thing? That woman at Coralee's was breathing fire at him the other night at dinner."

"My working theory is that he was doing some shady fertility business and Damari found out."

"Then he killed her to keep her quiet."

"And who killed him? An angry patient?" He wasn't convinced that Dan killed Damari.

"Maybe that Chinese woman or her husband."

"I'm sure the police will start with them. Hey, if you wanted to keep drugs hidden here and didn't want to keep them locked and accounted for, where in the hospital would you hide them?"

"Come on, buddy, I know you only work part time but if you need the money there are better ways."

Henry swatted Pat on the head. "Where would you hide fertility drugs that you didn't want everyone to know about?"

"If he was doing fertility treatments, they'd expect him to be signing them out."

"Then why was he ordering from Mexico?"

"Don't know. In any case, they'd need to be refrigerated. Let's get some help here. Skyler down in pharmacy is a buddy of mine. You know who he is, right?"

"Yeah. He's in charge of the hospital pharmacy."

"Let's see if Dr. Dan was legitimately signing out infertility hormones."

Henry followed Pat down to the pharmacy, which was around the corner from the morgue. Skyler, a young Ryan Gosling look-a-like, sat at his computer. He swiveled around when the door opened.

"Hey, Pat. I just refilled the candy drawer. Help yourself. You too, Dr. Fox. What do you need?"

Pat grabbed a Twix bar from the drawer and tossed a second one to Henry.

"My buddy Henry and I are looking for some info. Can you check the records and see if Dr. Fischer signed out fertility drugs over the past few months?"

Tyler tapped a few keys. Pat ate the candy bar, then grabbed a small bag of M&Ms from the drawer. Henry stared at the screen while Skyler worked.

"Yeah, he did. Nothing unusual. Looks like he had a handful of patients on them."

"Looks like the correct amount?"

"Yeah. Like I said, nothing sets off a flag here."

"Thanks, buddy."

"He must have an office fridge," said Henry. His words echoed in the empty, shiny corridor. "If he was getting what he needed right from the hospital pharmacy, why was he buying the same drugs from Mexico?"

"They'd certainly be cheaper. Do you think he had other patients who weren't registered with the hospital?"

"For what purpose? Was he augmenting the dosages?"

"Come on. I have a few minutes. Let's see what we can dig up."

Henry followed Pat to the elevator and up to Dan's office, where a custodian had propped the door open. Pat moved the 'Caution Wet Floor' sign down the hall and motioned for Henry to follow, pulling the door shut behind him.

"Here's the fridge. Let's take a look." Pat pulled the handle. "Waters, some expired yogurt, Reese's Peanut Butter Cups..."

"What's in the back?"

Pat reached in. "Some sort of leftovers in this Styrofoam container. Be my guest. And a box of raisins."

"Raisins? Look inside."

Pat opened the box and reached in. "Just raisins, no vials of fertility drugs."

"This was fruitless."

"Not the right choice of words. Technically, raisins are fruit." He tore open the package of Peanut Butter Cups. "Here. These will just go to waste." He popped one in his mouth and handed the other to Henry.

"Now what?"

"Let's have a look." He opened the desk drawers and rummaged through.

"Feel under the drawers," said Henry. His friend Susan Wiles taught them that trick.

"Nothing."

"Then see if there's a false bottom. Here, let me try." Henry felt around. "See, there's something behind this drawer." He pulled it off the tract and turned it upside down, dropping pens and staples on the floor. Taped to the back, was a small, black book. "Bingo."

"Well, well. What do we have here?"

Henry flipped through. "It's names, dates, and dosages. Look, here's Li Min, and what was the name of that patient who died from the overdose?"

"Riley or Reina—something with an *r*."

"There's a Ruth, and a Regine."

"Regine sounds familiar."

"These look like standard doses, nothing crazy. He's got half a dozen first names here. I wonder if any of them actually became pregnant."

"We know Regine and Li Min didn't. We can check his patient list and find out about the others. I'll bet his nurse knows."

Henry took out his phone and took a picture of the pages. Then he flipped to the back of the book. "There are several addresses here with tally marks and dates beside them. I wonder what that means?"

Pat looked at the entries and shrugged his shoulders. "You got me." Then he rifled through the papers on the desk. "Hey, look at this, buddy." He pulled a letter from an envelope he found under one of the piles. "Justice will be done if I die trying. Something about he knows it wasn't an accident." He skimmed the page. "Even though the courts didn't agree, I hold you responsible and will not let this go."

"What's the name?" asked Henry.

"Sean Mercer."

"Sean Mercer? Remember Dan was involved in a snowmobile accident last winter? I read the films."

"Yeah, he was hobbling around on crutches for a while."

The door opened, and a nurse stepped in. "Can I help you, Dr. Fox?" She discretely wiped her eyes with a tissue from the top of the desk. "I was looking for any new files that might be in here. I'm facing the tough job of calling his patients and breaking the news. I'm referring them to the new resident that just started. Dr. Jules is working on reducing his caseload since he plans to retire next year, but maybe in a pinch he can handle any complicated cases."

"Are there many of those? Complicated cases?" asked Henry.

"Not really," said the nurse. "Pretty much routine around here. I can't believe Dr. Dan is gone. He was so good to his patients and treated me and the other nurses like we mattered." She blew her nose. "Can I help you find something?"

"Dr. Fischer had a new drug he was trying out. He had asked me to consult on the side effects. I was wondering if it was in here."

"Why would it be? He'd have it locked up with all the others on this floor."

"It was still experimental so he may have kept it separate. Where else could he have kept it refrigerated?"

"I'd start with our floor storage. Come on." She led them to a room behind the nurses' station, then pulled out a key. "What exactly are you looking for?"

"Fertility drugs," said Henry.

"Nothing's listed." The nurse rummaged through the medications. "I don't see anything like that. There's a carton of Pitocin and antibiotics, that's all."

"Where else might we look?"

"He spent some time in labor and delivery and kept some meds up there. Then there's always the doctor's lounge. There's a fridge in there."

Henry stared at her, wondering about the possibility.

"I'm kidding. Your best bet is labor and delivery. I've got to go. Let me know if I can help you with anything else."

Pat straightened the pile and tucked the letter in his jacket pocket. "I'll give this to Megan when I see her later. Let's check labor and delivery." Pat led the way.

"Here we are." He got the nurse to unlock the cabinet, then foraged through.

The nurse, still holding the key, said, "Here's the inventory. These are the only drugs Dr. Fischer kept in here."

Henry scanned the list, then continued rifling through the cabinet. Convinced, he said, "Thanks. Let's go, Pat."

"Do you think he might have actually used the lounge fridge?" said Pat.

"It sounds crazy, but we can try." He opened the door to the lounge. "No one's in here." He opened the fridge and pulled out a carton. "Empty milk carton, a few apples. Hey, this looks promising." He opened a take-out carton.

"Well? Did you find something?"

Henry sniffed. "I think it's Kung Pao Chicken."

"This is a wild goose chase. I'd better get back to work."

"Wait! That takeout carton gave me an idea. Let's go back to Dan's office."

When they got back to the office, Henry opened Dan's fridge. He took out the Styrofoam container and sniffed. "It doesn't smell like leftovers." He opened the lid. "Unlabeled vials!"

"We can't be sure what's in those."

"But you have that friend in the lab who can help. The one who's always flirting with you."

"I'll drop it off. I'll be discreet."

"Let me know what Megan says about the letter you found. I'd better go back to work. Oh, and maybe Megan can interview the other patients listed in the little black book we found taped to the desk drawer. And Sean Mercer, the father of the kid who Dan had the snowmobile accident with."

Chapter 18

Emily finished her morning coffee at the kitchen table, while editing the previous day's writing. The table was half-littered with plates and dishes they'd removed from the cabinets. Somehow, sitting in the kitchen with the TV morning show playing in the background seemed less like work than sitting at her desk. She had envisioned spending all day all summer on her new book, but the allure of the present mystery pulled her in like a magnet. With the deadline fast approaching, she still hadn't finished the revisions of her current book her editor requested. Henry had left for the hospital, and Maddy was still asleep.

*Back to work.* She set aside the new book and pulled up the immediate task. She actually enjoyed the editing process, when she didn't feel rushed. Once the words were there on paper, she could relax and revel in the words, not worrying about keeping the facts and sequence straight. She'd lost track of time when there was a knock on the door.

"Hi, Dallas, come on in." He followed her into the kitchen. She scooped up her laptop and notes. "I'll get out of your way. Can I get you some coffee?"

"No thanks. Already had my limit for the day."

"That's right. I bet you were up half the night with Alexandra. Or is she sleeping through the night already?"

"Yeah, you were right the first time. Still wants her bottle a couple of times a night."

"I run on a lovely path down to the river. Lots of shade. You should tell your wife it's a nice place to take a stroller, and there's a little play area with toddler swings and a jungle gym. I guess she's too young for that."

"She gets around pretty good. She climbs up on the dresser and gets into my wife's necklaces. Already likes to play dress up."

Emily had no idea at what age babies started doing that sort of thing. Then again, at the last baby shower she attended for her work colleague, she remembered a basketful of safety latches and outlet plugs, so she supposed they got into things fairly quickly.

"Did you make any headway on the clues we found?"

"We've looked at the first four. There's the clue about the river, then we think the clue about chimes could mean a church. I recognized the third clue as an excerpt from Thomas Gray's *Elegy Written in a Country Churchyard.*"

"This is only my second summer here, but on the way here I pass an old church down by the river. And there's a cemetery next to it with an old-fashioned iron fence around it."

"That would be a great start. The fourth clue is a mish-mosh of letters." She put down the laptop and tore a sheet of paper from her notebook. "Does that mean anything to you?"

"Did you try unscrambling it? Or maybe each letter stands for something."

She scribbled some versions of letter arrangements. "Yeah, but doesn't ring a bell."

Dallas took the pen and scribbled. "Gre, Tad…"

"When I have time, I'll look at a map and see if any of those make sense. I've got to run by the college. Are you all set?"

"I'll finish clearing out the old cabinets today and I'll get measurements. By tomorrow I should be able to get the wood for you. Is there a Home Depot around here?"

"Yes, but that's silly. You'll get a better price from one of the local lumber mills. Ask Coralee. And I'll check with Henry. He's bought smaller amounts for some of his projects. Maddy's still asleep but she knows you'll be here."

Emily gathered her things and grabbed her keys. When she opened the front door, she realized she was blocked in by Dallas's van. The door was open, displaying an array of tools.

"Dallas, I can't get out of my driveway."

"Sorry. I should have parked along the road. Wasn't thinking."

He slid the door closed, jumped in the van, and pulled out of the driveway. Emily waved as she took off for St. Edwards.

In the mornings, she was usually able to get by with an open window in her Audi, but the humidity was particularly nasty today. She turned on the AC and resumed her audiobook. She pulled into the housing parking lot, listened to the end of the chapter, then went to see Li Min.

The office was as quiet as a graveyard and when the door creaked open, Li Min looked up from the book she was reading at the front counter.

"Emily, what can I do for you?"

Understandably, Li Min lacked the effervescence she'd had last time Emily visited this office. She took a lackadaisical swig from the thermos on the counter.

"At least now I can drink coffee."

"I'm so sorry. I know how excited you were about having a baby."

"I'm beginning to think it will never happen. We spent the last of our savings working with Dr. Dan. At least he got what he deserved. I'm not shedding any tears about his death."

"It sounds clichéd, but there are many ways to have a family. Look at Henry and me. We never expected to wind up adopting a teenager at our age, but what a blessing it's been."

"We can't afford private adoption. Especially not now."

"Li Min, did Damari have anything to do with Dr. Fischer's fertility enterprise? I've heard of college students selling their eggs for…"

Li Min laughed. "No way. Damari wouldn't even get a flu shot. She hated needles.

"Why were you convinced Dr. Fischer was your answer to getting pregnant? I mean, why not go to one of the big fertility clinics?"

"For one, the nearest one is four hours away, and you have to get shots daily and have bloodwork…it isn't feasible, not if you have a job you have to be at in a different town. And the expense. Insurance doesn't cover fertility treatments but Dr. Fischer found a way around it."

"Why would he do that?"

"He cared about his patients—or so he said."

"Did the police question you about Dr. Fischer's murder? I mean, there were all those witnesses who saw you getting angry at him at Coralee's that night."

"Do I look like a murderer? Come on. Besides, Shen and I both have an alibi. We stopped for drinks at Toby's Tavern. After all, it didn't matter anymore if I drank. There were plenty of witnesses. I'm not sure I like how you suspect me."

"I'm sorry. I didn't mean to come off that way. I've just gotten wrapped up in this whole thing. I'll let you get back to work."

Cared about his patients? Emily knew doctors were compassionate but to risk being linked to fraudulent insurance claims? There was too much at stake. She arrived home just as Jonathan was pulling into the driveway, behind Dallas's van.

"Perfect timing," said Jonathan. He followed her into the house.

"Don't mind all the banging. We're having new cabinets made. Let's sit out in the back yard. Where it's quieter."

"We got back the forensics report. The blood on the oar didn't belong to Robby, nor did they find his fingerprints. That's good news."

"Unless he wore gloves."

"If we're thinking crime of passion, it's unlikely he thought ahead. Besides, there weren't any gloves found at the crime scene or in Robby's room."

"Were you able to poke holes in any of the eyewitness reports?"

"As a matter of fact, I scoured the records from the interviews. Dan Fischer said he saw Robby at the picnic eating a hotdog."

"And?"

"Didn't Maddy say something about him being a vegan?"

"Of course! So Dan was lying about seeing him the day of Damari's murder!"

"And the fast food receipt? Would he have ordered a quarter pounder?"

"Someone planted it. Do you think it was Dan? Come to think of it, Dan was the one who found the lunchbox."

"I know he's dead, but I think we can build a case for Dan framing Robby."

"And killing Damari?" Emily hoped this would end Robby's nightmare.

"Nothing tangible but we'll keep looking. At least by showing Robby was framed, it gives us reasonable doubt."

"Henry thinks Damari may have caught on to Dan importing those fertility drugs and that's why he killed her."

"We're exploring all options," said Megan.

"What about the anonymous tips? Someone claims to have seen a boy in a red sweatshirt fleeing the crime scene. And the red hoodie found by the lake?"

"The key word is *anonymous*. Dan could have made that call." Jonathan stood up from the picnic table. "I'm going back to work on this."

Emily noticed the kitchen curtains blowing through the open window and wondered how much longer they'd be able to get away without running the A/C all day. She walked Jonathan out to his car, then went back inside where there was a lull in the cacophony in the kitchen. She peeked in.

"Wow, it's looking good! I'm excited!"

"This wood looks lovely in here. Great choice. Feel this." He pulled a drawer open and closed. "Hear anything?"

"No! It's smooth as glass. I won't miss jiggling the drawer back onto its track every time I pull out a spatula."

"I heard your lawyer friend come in. Did he clear your daughter's friend?"

"He's working on it."

"Finding the murder weapon in the closet couldn't have been helpful. I heard there was blood on the oar. I wonder if it was his?"

"It wasn't. I'm sure it won't be long before they figure out who's blood besides the victim's it really is." She looked at the clock. "If you want to knock off a little early and take that baby of yours out to the park, go ahead. You did a lot today."

"I'll be back tomorrow, then. Another day or two and I'll be out of your hair."

Chapter 19

Emily took a quick shower, pulled her still damp hair into a stubby ponytail, and put on a pair of baby blue capris with a gauzy, embroidered top. She'd been thinking about the clues, and along with what Dallas said about the graveyard, was convinced it was worth investigating. Henry would be working late and agreed to meet them at the inn for dinner, but not for a few hours. She knocked on Maddy's door.

"Feel like going on a scavenger hunt? What do you say we swing by the cemetery before dinner?" The words rolled out of her mouth as casually as if she'd just asked Maddy to stop at the grocery store with her.

"Do you think we'll find something?"

"We've got the quote from Gray's *Elegy Written in a Country Churchyard*, chimes, and river. The old cemetery, behind the old church, isn't far from the river."

"What about that mish mosh of letters? We haven't unscrambled it yet."

Surprised Maddy wasn't more eager, she said, "We don't have to, it was just a thought."

"No, I want to. It'll keep my mind off Robby sitting in a jail cell. I can be ready in ten minutes."

Emily had run by the river before, but not near the church. When they pulled up next to it, the grass in front was overgrown and a piece of board hung half off the roof at the base of the steeple.

"I wonder if there are chimes up in that bell tower," said Emily. She felt like she was on the set of a horror movie as she made her way up to the wooden church door, but then again, her imagination was always in overdrive. "It's locked."

Maddy whispered over her shoulder. "That padlock is so rusty, I bet we can hack through it."

"With what? The nail clipper in my purse? We need a real tool for that. Besides, I'm pretty sure that would be considered trespassing. Look at the placard. It's an official historic building."

"What about the cemetery? No one says we can't walk around outside, right? Come on."

Emily followed her daughter around the outside of the church. The back was a mess of weeds and fallen branches.

"I'm wearing my new sandals," said Emily. "And there may be snakes or spiders in there for all we know." Whose idea was this, anyway?"

"We're here now. I'm wearing sneakers. I'll go." She waded through the grass and weeds to the rusty, iron fence surrounding the churchyard. Again, a rusty padlock guarded the area. She pulled on it, but it wouldn't budge. Then she tried climbing the fence.

"Maddy, get down before you get hurt!" She heard the thud before the words finished leaving her mouth. "Are you okay?"

In the few seconds delay before her answer, Emily couldn't breathe. Then she watched Maddy get up and brush the leaves off her shorts.

"I'm fine. Looks like no one's been here for a hundred years. There are weeds everywhere."

"Can you climb back out?" Although it was still daylight, this place gave her the creeps. She half expected dancing skeletons or a ghost to jump out from behind a grave stone.

Maddy leaned down and cleared away one of the headstones as best she could. "Do you think there's treasure buried beneath one of these graves? Is that why the clue led us here?"

"I can't imagine why Henry's grandfather would have buried treasure here and not in his own back yard. If there was a treasure, that is. Come on, I'm hungry"

Maddy boosted herself over the iron fence. "You don't have to hold onto me, Emily. I'm a big girl." She jumped to the ground.

Emily had a flash of what it would have been like to watch Maddy ride her bike for the first time. How hard it would have been to let go, knowing she could fall. How hard it was to be in charge of protecting someone and failing to live up to the job. Beth. She shook off her thoughts before beating herself up again.

"Emily, did you hear me?"

Maddy's voice brought her back to the present. "No, what did you say?"

"Let's come back tomorrow with some tools."

Not convinced, she nodded her head and unlocked her Audi. Maddy had her monster headphones on, with her phone in her lap. She couldn't help but think how things had come full circle, from the oversized headphones in vogue when she was a teenager, to the micro-earbuds of the recent past, and back to super-sized. Of course, those expensive Dr. Beats she and Henry bought for Maddy's birthday were wireless. They drove silently to the inn to meet Jonathan Stirling for dinner. Was Maddy sleeping, or just enjoying the music with her eyes closed? She tapped her shoulder. "We're here."

Maddy jumped. "I can hear you, you don't have to shout."

Jonathan, in a crisp, green polo shirt with his hair neatly combed, was already seated when they arrived.

"Glad you called," said Jonathan. "I hate eating alone."

The dining room at the inn was buzzing with summer visitors, but Coralee always managed to seat them, even at the last minute.

Maddy said, "Have you seen Robby? Is he doing okay?"

"He's a little more optimistic now that we're going with the theory he was framed. I showed him the photo of the sweatshirt. It's missing the drawstring and he says it's his, but has no idea how it got on that path. He says he has no enemies in town—keeps to himself most of the time."

"He's really kind of shy. Other than Damari, he never mentioned friends."

They had barely been seated when Henry walked in. "Sorry I'm late. Got a call when I was about to leave the hospital. The fertility drugs we found in Dan's office fridge contained a fraction of the hormones they were supposed to have. Now the question is, if Dan was using those on his patients, what was he doing with the legit ones he signed out from the hospital pharmacy?"

Jonathan put down his glass of water. "Could he have been selling them?"

"To whom? Any doctor in his right mind wouldn't be buying black market drugs, and patients themselves wouldn't know what to do with them."

Coralee brought fresh baked bread to the table. "I heard Dallas is almost finished with your kitchen. How's it looking?"

"Beautiful."

"Told you the man does good work. He's got a few more guest rooms to update for me when he's finished. His poor wife. She's sitting cooped up with a baby, while he's spending hours working. I'm sure that isn't what she bargained for, but trying to feed a family on a teacher's salary? It's no wonder he's picking up every odd job he can get his hands on."

"Does she ever come around here?" Emily put her menu down.

"No. From what Dallas has said, his wife's a bit of a germaphobe and doesn't like bringing the baby near crowds of people. You know first time moms."

Emily really didn't, but imagined if she'd had Maddy as a baby she would have wanted to show her off to everyone.

"Maybe he'd rather be here than changing diapers and listening to crying," said Henry.

"Or perhaps Lisa is depressed and doesn't want to go out. I hate to say it, but after I had Noah, I was so depressed I thought about ending it all."

Emily said, "No way. You're always so upbeat."

"Hormones and chemical imbalances can't be overcome by an upbeat personality. I thought about killing myself. I even counted the pain pills the doctor gave me after the C-section. I thought about crushing them up and chugging them with a bottle of beer."

Emily's jaw dropped. "In a million years, I can't picture it. What turned things around for you?"

"A friend from my high school days called to congratulate me on the baby. I hadn't talked to her in months, but her timing was right on. Uncanny. She asked if everything was okay. She said I sounded sad. That's when I opened up to her about how I was feeling. She convinced me to get help."

"And you talked it out with a therapist?"

"Talking came afterward. First, the doctor got me on anti-depressants. I felt like such a failure having to take meds when I had a new baby at home and everything to live for. He explained it wasn't my fault and that much mental illness was simply a matter of out of whack brain chemicals. In my case, it was postpartum depression. Pregnancy does a number on your hormones."

"So you took the pills and you were fine," said Maddy.

Henry interjected, "It's not that simple. It takes a while for the medication to build up and start working."

"True, but I hung in there until the black curtain lifted." Coralee went around the table taking orders. Although she had servers to do that, she couldn't help being hands-on with her guests. Emily knew that personal touch added to the inn's tremendous success. She had a new sense of admiration for Coralee, first for getting help when she needed it, and second for having the courage to talk about it.

Jonathan said, "Henry, back to those drugs. Do you think he was selling the legit ones off to the highest bidder and substituting the watered down versions?"

Emily said, "I read something about women in India being paid to be surrogates. Suppose they imported the drugs? Or some similar scenario in another part of the world."

Henry remembered the addresses in the black book he and Pat found taped to the bottom drawer in Dan's office. Weren't a few of those international? "Yes! I'll bet that's it. Pat gave the book to his detective girlfriend. I'll let her know our theory."

"Back to Robby," said Maddy. "If he's being framed, someone had to have taken his sweatshirt and lunch box to plant them. And why Robby? Is he the only one in town someone imagined would have a motive?"

"It had to be someone who knew they were together." Emily ran through the list. Li Min, her husband, Dan…"

"And, that knew they broke up," added Maddy.

"Henry, wasn't it Dan who suggested that golf outing? Isn't that where the lunch box was found?"

Henry said, "That's right. And now that we know the drugs were watered down for sure, my best guess is that Damari found out and Dan went after her to keep her quiet. He may have played the part of being interested in her just to find out what she knew."

"Or to make sure she stayed quiet," said Jonathan. "He very well could be the one who planted the lunch box."

"And then what? Someone turned around and killed Dan and it had nothing to do with the first murder?" Emily grabbed another piece of bread.

"Could be a coincidence. Dan had enemies—his dissatisfied patients, the father of the kid killed in the snow mobile accident..."

"Henry, can you get me more information on that accident? It's worth exploring."

"Sure. I'll send it to you in the morning when I get to the hospital."

"I think we're looking at proving Dan Fischer killed Damari, then looking at who wanted Dan dead. Two separate cases," said Jonathan.

Chapter 20

Henry dropped by the morgue before starting his shift the next morning.

"Pat, Dan mentioned he hired Robby to cut his lawn, remember? And Robby said he took his lunchbox with him on jobs. Do you think..."

"That Robby left his lunchbox at Dan's and Dan planted it?"

"Yeah. And maybe Robby left his red sweatshirt lying around, too. Or at least Dan knew he wore a red sweatshirt, picked up one at Walmart, and planted it." Henry paced around the office while he worked out his thoughts.

"How could we possibly prove either of those things? We know a gray-haired man was spotted at the lake with Damari the night she died. And it wasn't Professor Carlson, because the police have footage of him getting gas on the other side of town that night."

Pat's phone vibrated on his desk. "It's Megan."

"I'll leave you to talk. I need to get upstairs anyway."

Henry pushed the elevator button for the ground floor, then hit three deciding to check in on Chauncey first. His wife was sitting at his bedside. The room smelled of lavender, and Henry spotted a small tea candle lit on the nightstand. He was about to tell her it was against hospital rules to light a candle in the room, but let it go.

"Any change?"

"None. I keep talking to him. I heard sometimes they hear ya even if they aren't awake."

"That's true. It certainly can't hurt."

"I was thinking about something that happened before the accident. Chauncey and I were out to dinner down town a few nights earlier, and Chauncey swore we were being watched. After dinner we went for a walk to do some window shopping, and Chauncey said he thought someone was following us. At one point Chauncey turned around real quick and he said he saw someone dart around the corner. A few minutes later, this van goes speeding by us."

"Did you tell the police?"

"I just remembered last night. My mind's been too jumbled with worrying about Chauncey, I forgot."

"Do you remember anything about the van or the driver?"

"It was a white van. I couldn't see the driver, but he was in a real hurry. Do you think Chauncey was right? Was someone following us?"

"I don't know, but you have to call the police right away and tell them."

On the way to the emergency room, Henry processed the extent of what Chauncey's wife just said. If someone was following them a few nights earlier, perhaps Chauncey was targeted, and it wasn't an accidental hit and run. Why Chauncey? It was hard to imagine him having any enemies.

He mulled over the implications while he tended to a toddler's bee sting, an elderly man's stomach pain, and a middle-aged woman's migraine. After that, things were quiet. So quiet, he could hear his own stomach rumbling. The bowl of oatmeal he'd eaten hours ago hadn't been sufficient.

He took a walk down the nearly deserted corridor to the vending machine, and weighed the choices—peanut

M&M's or a two pack of Nature's Valley granola bars. Glancing at his Fitbit, he opted for the granola bars, but when he examined the back of the package, he realized the candy would've been calorically the better choice. Examining the calories? When had he turned into his wife?

He tore open the package and headed back to his office. That's when he saw her. Sneaking out of Dan Fischer's locked office. She turned her head left, then right. Clutching her open cardigan against her waist with her elbow, she looked over her shoulder. He slowed and took purposely quiet steps while she locked the office door. Then, he broke the silence.

"What were you doing in there?"

The nurse jumped and let out a minor scream. "You scared me. I, um."

"Where did you get a key to this office? Should I call the police and tell them you were nosing around a crime scene?" Technically, it wasn't a crime scene, but he wanted to scare her into being truthful.

"I left something. I was trying to retrieve it, that's all. Please, don't call them."

"Left what?" Whether it was the fact that he was a doctor, or the tone of his voice, she deferred to his authority.

"Nothing, I…"

"You can tell me, or you can tell the detective." He took his phone out of his pocket.

"Don't. I was retrieving this." She pulled a pair of lacy, red panties from under the cardigan. "I don't want my husband to find out."

Now he recognized her. She hadn't been working there long. "You're married to Dr. McPhee, aren't you?"

"Yes. And I don't see the point of him finding out about me and Dan, especially now that Dan is gone."

"An affair? And you met here? Right under your husband's nose?"

"That's right. Are you the marriage police?" Her defensiveness seemed to outweigh her fear.

"Not my concern. No one around here suspected? Or did they cover for you?"

"I'd slip in during shift changes. And Wednesday evenings. I told everyone I went to a book club over in Oakbridge. Obviously, it's over now. Telling my husband would do nothing but hurt him."

Wednesday evenings. "You were seeing him last month?"

"Not that it's your business." She seemed to remind herself that she was at his mercy as far as being reported to the police, "but yes, every single Wednesday."

"What about Founder's Day? The big celebration was on a Wednesday."

"I went to the picnic and fireworks with my husband. Dan was there, with that receptionist who died."

"So he was seeing the receptionist as well?"

"No, he had some business with her, that's all. We met back at his office like always, later that evening."

"What time did you speak to them?"

"Aren't you being a tad nosy?" She cleared her throat. "Around 8:00."

Henry tried to remember what time Damari was killed.

The nurse looked up and down the hall, which was getting busier as they spoke. "Can I go now?"

"Yeah, but the police may have some questions for you."

"Having an affair isn't illegal."

"Not about that. Did Dan and Damari, the receptionist, happen to go down to the docks?"

"I don't know about her. *He'd* been fishing out on the lake. As a matter of fact, he was holding a small cooler and said something about going home and sticking the fish in his freezer before coming to the hospital. He said he had to work late, but that was for my husband's benefit. I knew what he meant."

"So you saw Damari and Dan together around 8:00. Then you met Dan back at the hospital, when?"

"It was before 9:00. My husband was going back to the hospital to check on a patient. We rode together, and then I said they asked me to cover because they were short-handed. Told him I'd get a ride home." She looked at her watch. "I have to get back to my floor."

"I won't say anything to your husband, but the detectives will be talking to you about the night of the murder. You may have been one of the last people to see Damari alive."

Chapter 21

Jonathan sat with Chester nuzzled beside him on the couch. "Henry, that was good work. Now we know Dan Fischer had an alibi for the time Damari was killed."

"Detective Megan went back to the eye witness report. The witness spotted Dan and Damari on the lake while it was still light out. They'd been fishing, but right afterwards is when they ran into that nurse and Dr. McPhee. The police found the cooler of fish in Dan's fridge at his house and he swiped into the hospital at 8:45 p.m. The timeline checks out. Dan left the picnic, dropped off the fish, and was back at the hospital by 8:45. He couldn't have killed Damari."

"That's good for Dan, but leaves one less suspect as Damari's killer. Not so good for my client."

Emily brought out sandwiches. "The kitchen is getting back to normal. Just waiting on the new cabinets to be sanded and stained. I made egg salad, and there's ham. Maddy should be back any minute. Abby is teaching her a few things about photography. She says she's a natural."

Jonathan reached for the egg salad. "We're left with no other viable suspects in Damari's murder."

Henry said, "Not necessarily. What if the same killer wanted both Dan and Damari dead? What if there was a motive that tied the two together?" He didn't verbalize it, for fear of upsetting Emily and Maddy, but Dan had warned him he himself was in danger. And what about Chauncey? Did someone have it in for all four them?

"What do Dan, Damari, and Chauncey have in common?" said Jonathan.

Emily said, "They all work at the hospital. Could it be that?"

"Lots of people are employed there," said Henry. "Why them, specifically?" *Why us specifically.*

"What other factors are we missing?" said Jonathan. "Did they go to the same church? Live in the same neighborhood? Where else did their paths cross?"

"How about the fertility drugs? Didn't you say, Henry, that maybe Damari found out Dan was replacing the hospital drugs with the weaker ones he imported from Mexico? Chauncey is a nurse. Maybe he knew it too."

"If and when he wakes up, we can ask."

Maddy opened the front door. "Hey, did you bring news about freeing Robby?" She put her camera and a stack of mail on the table by the door.

Jonathan put down his plate. "No, but we're getting closer. Let's assume the deaths are linked. Damari Cooper, Doctor Fischer, Chauncey the nurse—what's the common bond between the victims."

"If there's another motive, Robby would be off the hook, right?" asked Maddy.

Emily said, "You know Jonathan and the police are working on it. Trust them."

"Imagine if you were sitting in a jail cell with no money for bail. How would you feel, Emily? How patient would you be?" Maddy responded.

Jonathan said, "I've been bothered by the same thing, Maddy. After working with Robby, I'm convinced of his innocence. I have some investments I can access. I'm going to put up the bail money and get him out."

Maddy hugged him. "Really? You'd do that?"

Henry said, "Are you sure, Jonathan? It's a lot of money."

"He doesn't have any family around and he won't have the means to flee the country. He told me he doesn't even have a passport. I feel perfectly confident that my investment will be safe."

"With him out, maybe he'll remember something that will help clear him," said Emily.

"Thanks for lunch. I'm going to work on the bail right now. I'll call you when he's free."

Emily let him out and picked up the stack of mail. "Hey, Maddy. The results from *Ancestors Are Us* are here!"

After Maddy had been assigned to make a code of arms for school last year, Henry felt like she needed a connection to her past and had ordered the kit.

"Let me see," said Maddy. She grabbed the envelope from Emily and tore it open. "It's not too easy to understand."

Henry took it from her. "Well, it says you are 60% Scottish, which we knew, some more European, and Indian, as in from India."

"My father must have been from there, right?"

"At least he had Indian blood in him."

"I don't look a bit Indian."

"The percentage isn't that high. The genes from your mom's side dominated. And here's some good news. No risk factors for major diseases. Your mom had Huntington's in her family, but you're all clear!"

"Thanks for getting this for me, Henry. I can't believe it was so easy to find out. No blood drawn or anything."

"Amazing how much you can find out about someone just from a drop of saliva. Some cold cases have been solved after lying dormant for years now that we have this technology."

"Maybe the police will find some saliva from the actual killer and Robby will be off the hook. At least he's getting out of jail. Do you think Coralee will still let him live at the inn?"

"I'm sure she will. She's got a big heart and she went through having her own son in prison so she's been sympathetic all along."

"Hey, this has gotten me thinking about the clues. Emily and I went over to the old church down by the river. There's a rusty gate locked with a padlock, and an old graveyard. Can we go back and explore?"

"Emily, you didn't tell me…"

"It was on the way to dinner last night. Dallas came up with the idea of the chimes meaning the church by the river and the graveyard like in the poem Gray's *Elegy*."

"I'm off today. I suppose we could go look."

"Wear old clothes and closed shoes. It's an overgrown mess and there's a fence to climb over," said Emily. "Oh, and let's bring the skeleton key just in case it goes with the lock."

"We'll bring all the clues. I'll go get them," said Maddy. She retrieved the silver box and brought it to the coffee table. "Here's the key, and the poem. What about this playing card? It's an ace of spades."

"Don't know. Maybe when we get to the church it'll mean something. I'm going to throw on some jeans and my old running shoes. Maddy, why don't you do the same. You already scraped your knee last night climbing the fence."

After changing and gathering up the clues, they hopped into Henry's Jeep. The air was sticky and Emily hoped they'd beat the late afternoon rain which had become a pattern this summer.

"How long do you think it will be before Robby gets out?" said Maddy.

"Jonathan was going right over to the jail. I don't think it'll be long," said Emily.

"Can we invite him over to dinner when he gets out?"

"Of course," said Emily. "You can make Coralee's squash casserole. You still have the recipe, right?"

"It's in the kitchen drawer."

"I'll drag out that old ice cream maker we got as a housewarming gift." She turned around and saw a twinkle in Maddy's eyes. She had a feeling there was a crush going on and hoped beyond hope that Robby would be cleared.

Henry pulled onto the dirt path leading to the church. "Looks like no one's been here in a long time."

"Except for us. Come on," said Maddy. She hopped out and ran to the gate. "Give me the key."

Emily took it out of the box and handed it to Maddy. "Careful, there's a lot of rust."

Maddy tried to fit it into the lock. "It won't go in."

"Scrape it against the bars. Try to loosen the rust," said Henry.

"I'm trying." She turned it in different directions. "It doesn't fit. I think it's the wrong key."

"Plan B?"

"Plan B," said Emily. Before she got the words out, Maddy was halfway over the fence. Emily heard a thump, but this time Maddy had landed on her feet. "Come on."

Henry gave Emily a boost, then followed her over the fence. He was secretly proud that he and Emily still had the wear-with-all to hop fences and explore graveyards. Maybe they weren't as old as he was starting to imagine.

"Let's clear some of these graves." Maddy started pulling at the weeds.

Emily took a pair of gloves out of her pocket. "Put these on."

"I can't get these up."

Henry pulled with her. "I have some tools in the Jeep." He returned with a Swiss army knife and sawed at the weeds. "There, that works." He rubbed his sore hand on his shirt.

Maddy cleared the tombstone. "Margaret Hutchinson. Loving mother and wife. 1900-1929. Here's another one." She and Henry worked to clear another tombstone. "Elizabeth Raines. 1903-1904. She was just a baby!"

Emily, who was searching through the cemetery, said, "Back in those days, a lot of infants died of things that are curable now."

The Swiss army knife was frustratingly slow. Henry said, "Why don't we run home and get some real tools before it gets dark."

They jumped into the Jeep.

"I wonder when that church became abandoned?" said Emily.

"They might have records over at City Hall. I've often wondered why there wasn't a history museum in our town like the one over in Oakbridge."

"Yeah, that one is tiny but look at what we learned about Vermont and slavery when we visited."

He drove down the hilly road, back toward home. He wondered if his grandfather was trying to get him caught up on family history. He remembered a conversation he overheard as a little boy. His grandmother was fighting with his grandfather and said something about him being the black sheep of the family and hoping the grandkids never would know. When he walked into the kitchen, they stopped talking abruptly. Why had he kept that memory for so long? Something about the tone in which it was said... He had a feeling in his gut that they were about to find out something better left hidden.

"Henry, that's our turn," said Emily. "You were a million miles away."

"So it is. I'll run out and get some tools and a flashlight."

"Hurry, or it will be too dark to work," said Maddy.

Henry retrieved gardening shears and a saw from the barn. On the way back to the car, he noticed a stain in the driveway and bent down to inspect it. It felt like oil or gasoline, he couldn't be sure. Maddy rolled down the window and shouted, "Hurry, Henry."

He got back in the driver's seat. "Off we go."

The new tools were much more efficient than the Swiss army knife. They systematically worked through each row of the cemetery, hardly noticing how dark it had become. The sound of crickets broke the deadly silence.

Maddy shouted, "Look! This one says, 'Theodore Fox, 1910-1970. Devoted husband to Mary, father to Martin and Theresa'."

"That was my grandfather! His name was Theodore. I never knew he was buried here." *Why didn't I know I had ancestors buried right here in town? If my grandfather left this as a clue, he had to know he'd someday be buried here. I'll bet my grandmother is here too.*

"Maybe that's what the scavenger hunt is all about," said Emily. "Your grandfather wanted you to know your family history."

Maddy said, "And I'm getting to discover it along with you, just as if I've been part of your family all along. Let's keep searching."

"It's dark now. How about we come back tomorrow?" suggested Emily.

"I'd like to stay, but it's pretty hard to see what we're doing here." Maddy followed Henry and Emily into the Jeep.

"I'll bet the clues all have something to do with your family. How about the chimes? Do you think it just was the graveyard, or something in the church?"

"You're guess is as good as mine. Like I said, my grandfather loved puzzles. I'm wondering about the playing card. When we get home, let's look at it more closely."

Henry pulled out onto the dirt road and started for home. It was drizzling, and he deliberately tried to slow down.

"Henry, what's wrong?" said Emily.

"It's the Jeep. I'm trying to slow down, but the brakes aren't working!" He headed down a winding hill, fighting to keep the car on the road."

"Careful, Henry. Can you pull over?"

"How?" There's no shoulder and gravity is making this worse as we speak."

"Are we going to die?" asked Maddy.

"Don't be so dramatic. Henry has this under control."

Henry clutched the steering wheel and jammed down as hard as he could on the brake. He fought to hold the Jeep on the road. He turned around a bend, barely missing the guardrail. Sweating, he was keenly aware that he held the life of his family in his hands. Maddy screamed from the backseat. Emily took out her phone but it fell out of her hands when they whipped around the last turn.

"Henry, watch out!"

He heard his wife's words in slow motion as the Jeep tumbled over the guardrail. The last thing he felt was the airbag smacking him in the face as the car rolled over.

Chapter 22

Henry opened his eyes. Well, one of them anyway. The other throbbed and as hard as he tried, he couldn't get past seeing through a slit. Not that he could see much of anything in the dark. He tried to pull his left arm from where it was wedged against the door. It wouldn't budge. He wriggled the other arm free. *Emily!*

"Emily, are you okay? Emily, wake up!"

She felt like a limp sack of flour. His seatbelt kept him from fully embracing her. The tools he'd brought to the graveyard would be helpful. Too bad they were stashed in the back. *The tool.* Emily had bought them both seatbelt cutters/window smashers after watching a segment on Dr. Oz. He reached under the dashboard and was able to wriggle it out.

"Emily." He used the blade and after a short struggle, freed himself, and pulled out his other arm. "Emily." He stroked her gently, not knowing the extent of her injuries. What if he'd killed her?

"Maddy!" How had he forgotten, even for a moment, that he had a daughter in the back seat? He reached over the seat, feeling blood. He had to get them out of here. Emily moaned.

"Emily, are you okay?" He unclasped her seatbelt, then reached over to open her door. The driver side door was jammed. He couldn't feel his left leg, but pulled himself carefully over his wife and out the door.

"Henry, where am I?"

He cradled her neck and back, then lifted her to the ground beside the car. "We had an accident. It's going to be okay."

"Maddy! Where's Maddy?"

He was regaining feeling in his left leg, and hobbled to the passenger door. "It's stuck."

"You have to get her out. Is she moving? Is she…"

"I can't see much of anything." He went back in through Emily's door and carefully lifted Maddy to freedom. He leaned over and felt her chest rise and fall. "She's alive. Maddy, wake up!"

Emily tried to sit up. Her head throbbed and she felt as if she would throw up if she continued. "How will anyone find us? Does your phone work? Mine's in my purse, in the car."

Henry felt his pocket. It must still be in the car. He hobbled back to the car, and reached around. "I can't find it."

"Henry, do you smell something?"

His heart sank. *Smoke.* With urgency driven by the memory of Dan's car accident, he came back out, carefully picked up Maddy, and carried her as far from the car as possible.

"Henry, what's going on?"

He said, "If you grab my arm, can you walk?"

She now knew where the expression 'seeing stars' came from. "I think so." When she stood up, she vomited. Henry wiped her face with the bottom of his shirt.

"Come on." He put his arm around her waist and led her away from the car. He definitely smelled smoke now. Frustrated, he picked her up and hustled as best he could to where he'd put Maddy.

"Henry, we have to get an ambulance. It's dark and I'm scared. No one will look over the guard rail and see us."

Henry's head throbbed. If he went back to the car to search for a phone, he may get caught in an explosion. If he waited, Maddy might die of her injuries. Then, he though he heard sirens. Was it his imagination?

Emily shrieked. "I think it's an ambulance or a fire truck."

He heard it now, breaking through the silence and lighting the darkness. The EMT's ran to them.

"You're going to be okay. We're here."

"Go to my daughter. She's unconscious. How did you find us?"

"Lucky for you that car of yours has a GPS emergency system. It saved your life."

A fire truck whizzed by and headed to the smoking Jeep. One of the paramedics went to Emily.

"I'm fine, just help my daughter."

"That wrist looks broken." He shone a light in her eyes. "And I'm fairly certain you have a concussion. Let's get you and your family to the hospital."

The ride seemed interminable When they finally got to the hospital, Maddy was whisked into the urgent section of the emergency department. Emily and Henry were taken to treatment rooms, separated by a curtain.

"I'm a doctor. I'm fine. I need to be with my daughter."

The new resident said, "I know who you are, Dr. Fox. Let me check you over and you'll be free."

After being cleared with severe bruises and a soon to be black eye, Henry popped a few Ibuprofen and held an ice pack to his eye as he found Emily.

"My wrist is broken and I have a concussion," she said. "They want me to stay overnight but I don't want to."

Henry talked to the resident, who agreed to let her go after Henry promised to watch her carefully and bring her back to get a cast after the swelling subsided.

"Where's Maddy?"

"They took her to the OR. She had some abdominal injuries,"

"Will she be okay?"

Henry trembled. Not wanting to alarm his wife, he said, "She's in good hands. I'm sure she'll be fine." He led her to the waiting room.

"Henry, buddy, what happened? Are you okay? You look like you lost a fight with a heavyweight." Pat looked him over, then turned to Emily. "And you? Is the wrist broken?"

She ran her other hand over the ace bandage. "Yeah, but I'm fine. It's Maddy we're worried about."

Detective Megan came in. "I saw the accident report. Is everyone okay?"

Henry answered, "We think so. Maddy's in surgery."

"Tell me what happened? How did you lose control of the car?"

"The brakes went out. I'm not sure what happened. I do remember seeing oil in the driveway, or maybe it was brake fluid."

"I'll send someone by to test it. The car is pretty damaged, but we'll see what we can find."

Henry was reluctant to voice his concern. In the pit of his stomach, he felt as if this was done deliberately. Dan Fischer warned him that someone would be coming after him. He didn't want to admit what he felt was the truth. Someone wanted him dead.

Pat brought them Styrofoam cups of coffee and waited with them as Megan returned to the station to begin an investigation. After several hours, the surgeon appeared. Henry knew him, and tried to read his expression.

"Your daughter had abdominal injuries, which we were able to repair. She's stable, but the next 24 hours are crucial. She's in recovery now."

Henry held Emily's good hand and ran into the recovery room with her.

"Henry, she looks awful! What if we lose her? Fiona trusted us to take care of her and now."

"It's all my fault. I couldn't keep control of the car."

"And it was my idea to go to the cemetery in the first place."

Henry was still concerned about his wife's concussion. "Why don't we go home and get a few hours of sleep. They'll call the minute anything changes. She won't wake up for a while."

Emily kissed Maddy's forehead and followed Henry to the parking lot. Working on autopilot, they realized at the same instant they had no car!

Chapter 23

"Did you sleep at all?" asked Henry. He poured a cup of coffee and filled Chester's bowl. "Last text was an hour ago and there's been no change. How's your arm doing?"

"Hurts, but right now I'm more concerned about Maddy." She inspected his eye. "Don't go telling everyone your wife beat you."

"I'll say I walked into a door." He gave her a kiss.

"Is that your phone?"

Henry picked it up off the table. "No change as of last update. We're heading to the hospital now. What? You're sure? I see. I noticed a spot of oil in the driveway. I assumed it was oil. Brake fluid? I will."

"You will what? Who was that?"

"Detective Wooster. They were able to inspect the Jeep."

"And?"

"Someone tampered with the brakes. Someone is after me."

"What! First Damari, then Chauncey, then Dan, and now you? Are you saying there's a serial killer right here in Sugarbury Falls?"

"We have to connect the dots. What do we all have in common?"

"The obvious is that you all work or worked at the hospital. What about the fertility drugs? Dan was importing them from Mexico and swapping them with the full strength ones. Damari found out. You know…"

"What does Chauncey have to do with it? He worked in the emergency department and ICU. I don't think he and Dan would have crossed paths. And I didn't know myself until recently." Henry put his mug in the sink. "Let's go check on Maddy."

When they arrived at the hospital, they went directly to Maddy's room. The nurse told them that Maddy had been stable throughout the night, though she hadn't woken up.

"She looks so vulnerable and frail." Emily squeezed her hand, "Come on, honey. We're here. Wake up, please."

Jonathan, carrying a plant with a "Get well soon" balloon, appeared in the doorway. "May I come in? I'm so sorry."

"How did you know about the accident?"

"This town spreads information faster than butter melts on hot toast. I heard all about it at the inn during breakfast this morning. Henry, your eye looks awful. Are the two of you all right?"

"Yes, just worried about Maddy. She had surgery last night and hasn't woken up. She should be up by now." Emily rested her head on Maddy's chest, avoiding the tangle of wires she was connected to.

"I posted bail for Robby. Gave him a ride home to the inn this morning."

Emily lifted her head. "That's great news. He must be so happy to be out of there."

"Happy, but worried. He still has no alibi for the night Damari was killed. I'm going to get a list of the guests who were at the inn the night of the murder. The police interviewed them, but by now maybe they remember something."

"Her guests are from all over the country," said Emily.

"Just a phone call away. I'm going to get right on it."

After Jonathan left, Emily said, "Didn't you give a statement about the injuries in the Sean Mercer case?"

"I'd forgotten that. Yes, I think so. I write up the radiology reports if an accident happens while I'm working the ER."

"Did you find Dan Fischer to be at fault?"

"I don't think so. Let's go to my office and I'll check through the reports. The nurse will text us if Maddy wakes up."

He and Emily went into the office. "It'll take a few minutes." He turned on the computer.

"Could Damari and Chauncey have any connection to the snowmobile accident?"

"I suppose Chauncey may have been on duty, but if I remember correctly, Sean's son was dead on arrival. Let me look up my records."

Emily's arm itched beneath the bandage. She knew she'd have to make time to get a cast put on sooner rather than later. Maddy had made it through surgery, but she wasn't out of the woods by any means. How must Sean Mercer have felt when he heard his son was dead? How could you ever recover after losing a child? Her own mother never did.

"Emily, I found the report. Sean's son had broken bones, and a head injury consistent with falling off a snowmobile. I didn't say the injuries were made worse by high speed or anything like that. He was dead on arrival, like I thought."

"Call Megan. See if they used your records in court."

Henry called the police station, but Megan was unavailable. "I left a message." He watched Emily wince and hug her arm. "Come on. Let's get that arm looked at." Henry called his friend who was an orthopedic surgeon. He agreed to squeeze Emily in right away.

The waiting room was non-descript, and the receptionist immediately ushered them into a treatment room, earning glares from patients waiting amidst old magazines. Dr. Price was about Henry's age and they'd become friend's while doing the hospital fitness challenge last year.

The doctor looked at the x-rays from the emergency room, and carefully unwrapped her arm. "It's a simple break. If all goes well, we can get her out of the cast in 3-4 weeks."

Emily was relieved. She'd envisioned not running or swimming all summer long. "Thanks, doctor." Watching him apply the cold, wet pieces of gauze around her arm reminded her of the paper-maché Venus she'd helped Maddy make last school year.

"Come into my office and we'll discuss follow-up."

When they went into his office, Henry's attention was drawn to a family tree, framed behind the desk.

"Jim, did you trace your family like that?"

"Yeah, me and my wife. She's got her own hanging in our bedroom at home. We took on the project when she was pregnant with our first."

Henry looked at it more closely. "So your family has been here for generations."

"Yeah. We have records going back as far as the slavery era. Found a lot through the church records."

"What if the church no longer exists?" asked Emily.

"We looked in town hall basements, found cemetery maps, and my wife even talked to one of her descendants and found out a bunch. My wife became quite the expert if you're thinking of taking on such a project."

"Thanks," said Emily. "We may take you up on that."

Henry's phone vibrated. "It's a text from Maddy's nurse. Says it's an emergency."

Henry and Emily ran to the elevator. Emily's mind worked in overdrive. Was Maddy dead? Did she wake up? What was happening?

Henry drummed his fingers on the panel, as if he could make the elevator move faster. When it stopped on an in-between floor, he pressed the close door button a dozen times and shouted at those waiting.

"Catch another ride. This is an emergency." He felt adrenaline rushing through his body.

Finally, the door slid open. "Come on." He grabbed Emily's good arm and led her to Maddy's room. "What's wrong?" Beeps and alarms sounded.

A nurse said, "She's allergic to the antibiotic. There was nothing in her medical history."

*Medical history?* They knew very little about Maddy's medical history. Certainly not that she was allergic to this particular drug. A doctor asked him to stand back. A nurse injected something into Maddy's IV. Henry fought to get closer.

"We've got this. Stand back and let us do our job," said the doctor.

Emily couldn't see much through the commotion. "What's happening? Is she going to be okay?" She heard the beeping subside to a hum. *Oh my God, is she dead?*

"It's okay. We've got this under control. She's going to be okay," said the doctor. "You should get whatever medical history you can."

"We adopted her and her mother is dead," said Emily.

"What about her biological father?"

Emily squirmed. "He was an anonymous sperm donor."

The nurse said, "Look, her eyes are open!"

Emily pushed through to the bedside. "Maddy, Maddy, can you hear me? It's Emily."

Maddy groaned and pointed to the water pitcher on the night stand. "Can she have water?"

The nurse poured a bit into a glass and bent a straw to Maddy's mouth. "Just small sips."

The doctor examined her and reassured them that Maddy had turned a corner. He was, as he put it, 'cautiously optimistic'.

"You need to let her get some rest."

Relieved, Henry and Emily kissed Maddy and said they'd be back.

A faint, hoarse voice uttered, "Robby."

"Jonathan posted bail and Robby is home at Coralee's. It's all good," said Emily.

Chapter 24

Emily and Henry spent the rest of the day at the hospital, visiting briefly with Maddy whenever she was awake. Henry suggested going home to get dinner after the nurse assured them Maddy's fever was down and her vitals strong.

Trying to convince Emily to leave, he said, "Chester needs his dinner. And he's been alone all day."

Emily slowly stood up, kissed Maddy, and assured her they'd be back soon.

Henry couldn't remember the last time he'd driven Emily's Audi. He fiddled with the mirrors and adjusted the seat back and forth. He'd have to think about replacing the Jeep very soon.

Back home, Henry said, "Don't forget to take the pain killers the doctor gave you." He foraged in the kitchen for a glass, annoyed at the disorganization. "When will this cabinet project be complete?"

"He's almost done. Dallas said he has a few more things to do but will be finished by the end of the week. Is someone at the door?"

Pat and Megan came in with a foil covered pan.

"You didn't have to make food," said Henry.

"Make? We picked it up from Coralee's. Figured the last thing you'd want to do is cook," said Pat.

Megan said, "Henry, I checked on the statement you asked about. It was presented in court by Dan's lawyer and helped convince the jury that the injuries would have happened in spite of Dan's speeding."

"So, is that motive? Is Mercer getting revenge for his son's death? Why now?"

"The high school graduation occurred a few weeks ago. The Mercer boy should have been on that stage getting a diploma. We think that could have been a trigger, *if* Sean Mercer is responsible."

"Did you find any connection to Damari or Chauncey?"

"Chauncey, no. Damari, however, was a witness. She and her friend were out snowmobiling the same day. The friend was in the restroom at the time, but Damari saw the whole thing."

"And she testified?"

"She testified at the trial that Dan wasn't going over the speed limit and Mercer's kid was the one who was speeding."

"Then it makes sense. Have you arrested Mercer?"

"We have to gather real evidence before we can do that. We'd have to place Mercer at the crime scenes. It's going to take some time."

Pat said, "But you forgot to tell them that Mercer drives a white Kia Sorrento."

"The eye witness reports were all over the place in Chauncey's hit and run. White van, or SUV, or one witness said it was a blue Honda Civic!"

"Okay, but it's more than we had before. At least we have an alternate motive for Damari's death. Jonathan is going to re-interview the guests who stayed at Coralee's the night of the murder. I can't believe no one can give Robby an alibi," said Emily.

"Well, try to rest that arm, Emily. Ron and I will aggressively follow the new lead."

"See you in the morning, buddy. Emily, take care of yourself."

After they left, Henry served the vegetable lasagna and poured them both a glass of wine. He couldn't help getting distracted by the almost finished cabinets and began thinking about the silver box. They were on to something now that they found his grandfather's tombstone. He didn't want to bring Emily back to the cemetery with her broken arm, but wondered if they could follow any of the other clues.

"Emily, I was thinking about our little scavenger hunt. The clue about the chimes—do you think it was only a hint for finding the graveyard?"

"I don't know. I'm assuming that was your grandfather's church if he was buried there. I don't know how to interpret the river clue. It's way too vague."

Henry ran to his desk and grabbed the box of clues. "Maybe he and my grandmother were married in that church and that's what he was trying to tell us. How can we find the marriage records?"

"When we moved in here after your parents died, we packed up a bunch of their things to donate and store."

"We gave away a bunch of old clothes and some furniture, right? That won't help us."

"But we stashed a box or two of personal items. We found your old track trophies, some photo albums…"

"We stored them up in the crawl space!"

"I'm thinking it's our best bet at finding family connections."

Henry finished the last bite of lasagna, then followed Emily up the loft. She was a bit unbalanced with the new cast and he'd be her safety net. He stood on their bed and pulled the cord for the crawl space. Steps dropped down.

"Voila!"

"Henry, be careful. No one's been up there for years." She opened the drawer in her nightstand and handed him a flashlight.

Henry coughed and rubbed his eyes. It smelled like moth balls and there wasn't enough space to stand up. There were boxes of things, some of which he and Emily stored; others that had been there for God only knew how long. He opened one that he and Emily had packed and found a yearbook, an old fashioned typewriter, and some framed photos. Then he opened a second one. Photos of his own parents, holding a baby. Him. They'd spent their summers here as long as he could remember.

"Did you find anything?"

"Just the memorabilia we packed away."

"Go to the back. Open the crates that were there when we moved in."

Henry let out a sneeze. The crates were nailed shut.

"Emily, can you grab my toolbox. I need something to pry open these crates."

While he waited, he could only imagine what might be in those boxes. He'd forgotten they were here. *What happened to the mementos Fiona collected when Maddy was a baby? Or when she started elementary school?*

"Here you go." Emily handed him a large screwdriver. He tried breaking through the slats and unscrewing the nails, but neither worked well.

"Did you get it?"

"It's harder than you think, prying open crates that have been nailed shut for decades." He propped up the flashlight and used both hands to pull.

"Did you open it?"

"Yep." Henry lifted out the things he found. First, a china doll wearing a lace dress. He didn't have a sister, so he assumed it belonged to his mother or his grandmother. He found a wooden pull toy, a Chess set, badminton birdies, and lawn darts. Maddy might enjoy badminton, when she gets out of the hospital.

"Well?"

"Just some toys."

"Try another one."

Did she realize how hard it was to open the first one? He used the same technique of prying off the lid with the screwdriver, and managed to open a second crate.

"There's just more toys." He shined the flashlight around the crawl space. "Wait, I see some kind of a trunk."

"Can you open it?"

He jammed the screwdriver between the trunk and the latch. "Got it."

"Well?"

"An old photo album. The pictures are faded, not in good shape at all. Oh, and here's a bible." He opened it up. It was heavier and larger than the bibles he'd seen. He handed it down to Emily, who cradled it with her good hand.

"We may find some records in there. What else do you see?"

He shined the flashlight into the trunk. "Some old newspaper clippings. I'll bring them down."

He's knees were sore from searching and he was happy they had something that might help. When he was back in the bedroom, he pushed the steps up into the ceiling and pulled it shut. When he returned from washing his dusty hands, he found Emily on the bed looking through the bible.

"Just as I thought! Families used to keep records in their bibles. I found birth and death dates as well as marriages and baptism certificates! It'll take a while to read through, especially since they are a bit smudged."

They read through what they could, finding an entry for Henry's grandparents' marriage. Emily was able to read the name of the church. "They weren't married where your grandfather is buried," said Emily. "I wonder if this church still exists and has chimes."

Henry read the entry. "That's the old white church in the town square, I think. We can check it out tomorrow." He glanced at the alarm clock on the nightstand and was surprised how late it was. "You should get some rest. I'm pretty tired myself."

Chapter 25

Emily woke up and checked her phone. 3 a.m. Too early to get up, and too late to easily fall back asleep. Her arm ached. She popped a few Ibuprofen into her mouth and turned on the small desk light. Those newspaper clipping were calling her. What was it they wanted to preserve?

The yellowed paper smelled of moth balls. She slipped on her reading glasses. The first article was about the 'new' tax laws that were taking effect. It was on the first page, and included a photo of townspeople holding protest signs in what she recognized as the town square. *Henry's grandparents were farmers. What were they protesting?*

The Industrial Revolution was getting started about this time. She looked more closely at the signs. *No factories welcome.* She supposed the farmers were trying to keep the competition away. Or were the factories after their land?

"What are you doing up?"

"I was trying not to wake you. I couldn't sleep."

"What are you reading?"

"This is an article that looks like the farmers were protesting the new factories which were trying to move in."

"My grandfather wasn't a farmer. He ran a lumber mill. I suppose big business would have been a threat."

She rifled through the articles. "Look. This is about a business tycoon who people thought was overtaking Sugarbury Falls. And look at the name."

Henry held the paper close. "Charlie Rivers! Maybe that's the river grandfather was referring to in the clue." He read on. "This man was a millionaire business tycoon. It says here he was turning New England into his personal monopoly."

Emily leafed through the other papers. "Wait a minute. Charlie Rivers went missing. His body was never found. Looks like your grandfather collected articles about his death."

"This is getting more and more intriguing."

"At least we have something to go on. We can research Charlie Rivers in the morning. I wonder if they eventually found out what happened to him."

Emily turned off the light and they both crawled back into bed, Chester still asleep between the two pillows. With the cast, it was hard to find a comfortable position. She tossed and turned the rest of the night trying to piece together clues about Damari's murder and clues regarding Henry's grandparents. Every time her mind quieted, she thought about Maddy alone in the hospital.

When she woke up, Henry had already gone downstairs.

"Did you make us breakfast?"

"Did what I could in this obstacle course. Eggs and toast." He was working on the Sudoku from the morning paper. "I checked in with the hospital. Maddy's fever is gone and she slept through the night. Want to head over when you finish eating?"

"Of course." She silently said a prayer of thanks while she sipped her coffee. Her phone vibrated. "It's a text from Jonathan. He wants us to stop by his room. Says it's important."

With the cast, driving was difficult if not impossible for Emily. Henry took the wheel of her Audi. At least replacing his Jeep at this moment wasn't an issue.

They'd get something before Emily went back to work in the fall. As he drove, he daydreamed about the possibilities. Exactly how much would a new Tesla cost? Or a Jaguar?

He pulled into the parking lot and opened the door for Emily. They met Jonathan in the dining room.

"Want some breakfast? This is the best blueberry French toast I've ever had."

"We ate. Tell us your news!"

"Robby has an alibi. He's off the hook. I checked with the company that makes his continuous glucose monitor. His blood sugar went low at 8:30 the night of the murder."

"That doesn't tell us where he was, does it?"

"No, but when I re-interviewed the guests who were here at the inn that night, one of them remembered something."

"What?" said Henry.

"An elderly man who was in the room next to Robby had gone downstairs to take a walk. When he came back into the lobby, he saw Robby. Robby was trying to find someone to get him juice but couldn't find anyone around. The man said Robby looked pale and didn't seem right. He had a can of Coke in his hand and offered it to Robby."

"Robby couldn't have told us this?"

"Says when his blood sugar goes low like that, it affects his memory."

"And how is the witness sure about the time?"

"He was heading back to his room to call his daughter who lives in California. He calls her at 5:30 every night, California time, just after she gets home from work. He says she worries about him living alone so they came up with this system."

Henry said, "The man's account is corroborated by the sensor data. He's clear, you're sure?"

"Charges have been dropped. And I got my bail money back."

"That's terrific news. We're on the way to the hospital. I can't wait to tell Maddy."

"I've got some packing to do. I figure I can make it back to New York well before dinner."

"And do you have dinner plans with anyone special?" asked Emily. She'd heard him talking to his girlfriend on the phone on more than one occasion.

"Yep. Plans with my special lady. I've really missed Janet. Might think about making things a little more serious."

"If there's a wedding, I hope we'll be invited."

"You betcha."

Noah, Coralee's son, came in with a cat carrier. "We had an extra one of these. Thought it might be helpful bringing Oreo home."

"Oreo?" said Emily.

"Jonathan, didn't you tell them?" said Noah.

"Now I'll have two special ladies in my life. I wound up spending some time in the cat café and every time I did, this beautiful tuxedo cat with a little bald spot would rub against my legs. Eventually, she worked her way onto my lap. I couldn't imagine leaving her here when I have a big, empty home back in New York."

"Wait till we tell Maddy. She'll be so happy for you both. We can't thank you enough for coming up here and helping Robby. Susan was right when she bragged about your skills."

"All in a day's work. Take care of that arm, Emily. Give my best to Maddy."

Emily made a mental note to call and thank her friend Susan for recommending him.

When they got to Maddy's room, she was sitting up in bed, sipping juice from a straw.

"Henry, your eye looks awful. Does it hurt?"

"Nah."

"Emily, is that a cast?"

"It's a simple fracture. I'll be out of the cast in just a few weeks. How are you feeling?"

"Sore, and I'm a little hungry. All they gave me for breakfast is juice and Jell-O."

Henry said, "It's because of the abdominal surgery. You'll be able to graduate to real food soon. We just saw Jonathan. He's adopting Oreo and taking her home with him."

"Home? He's leaving? Does that mean…"

"Maddy, we have the best news. The charges against Robby have been dropped! Jonathan did more digging and uncovered an alibi."

"That's great!" She winced and put her hand on her stomach. "I can't believe it's over."

"They still haven't caught Damari's killer, but yeah. For Robby, this whole nightmare is history."

Henry said, "Maybe we can bring him by later to visit." He didn't miss how her face lit up when he said that. His phone beeped. "It's from Megan. Says to come by the station. Maddy, get some rest and we'll be back later." He kissed her forehead.

When they got to the station, Megan ushered them into her office. "Henry, your report about speed not being responsible for the injuries Mercer's son died of *was* used in court. So was Damari's eyewitness account. Those two items swayed the decision to let Robby off the hook. Mercer was well aware of that."

"Then that's a link. What about Chauncey?"

"Haven't found a connection yet."

Emily said, "Do you have enough to arrest him?"

"Not even close at this point. We need physical evidence, or eyewitnesses placing him at the crime scenes. Be careful. There's something else."

"What?" said Henry.

"He has an arrest record. He beat up a guy in a bar fight back a few years ago, and his own wife filed a domestic abuse report."

Emily said, "Then your evidence shows he's violent."

"We don't have all the details, but I'm saying, be careful. We don't know what we're dealing with here."

Chapter 26

"Henry, please don't go over there. Megan says Mercer can be dangerous." They'd just gotten back home and Henry was grabbing her keys to go out again.

"I'm just going to talk to him, that's all. I'll be fine."

Emily's spine tingled as soon as he locked the door and she heard her Audi drive away. Henry was level headed and cautious—most of the time. *Don't worry. He's anything but impulsive and will leave if there's a risk.* She tried to concentrate on her writing, but between the painkillers and worrying about Henry, she couldn't. She missed running, which she was told to avoid while the cast was on. Maybe a walk would do her some good.

She started around the lake, and found herself heading to Rebecca and Abby's cabin. Rebecca was out front with Milo, cutting the grass.

"Hi, Rebecca. Want to do my lawn next?" She shouted behind her. "Rebecca." Then she tapped her on the shoulder.

Rebecca turned off the mower and whipped around braced to attack. When she saw Emily, she pulled earphones out of her ears. "Don't do that. I almost slugged you one."

Emily's thoughts on Rebecca's dubious work were reinforced. "Sorry, I didn't realize you were listening to music." *I'm lucky she wasn't carrying a concealed weapon.*

"How's the arm?"

"The painkillers work well."

"How about Maddy? When does she get out of the hospital?"

"Not sure, but she's doing much better. Robby was cleared of Damari's murder. She's happy about that."

"Great. So who's on the suspect list?"

"A guy named Sean Mercer is looking guilty. His son was involved in a snowmobile accident with Dan Fischer and he blames Dan for his son's death. Damari and Henry both gave accounts that cleared Dan. We are thinking that's the link."

"Come inside, it's getting hot out. Want some mango iced-tea?"

"Sure." She followed Rebecca and Milo inside. Milo ran to his water bowl, slurping and splashing water onto the floor, barely coming up for air.

"So what do the police have on this Mercer guy?"

"They say he was arrested in a bar fight, and there were charges of domestic violence. Do you think…"

Rebecca grabbed her laptop and started searching before Emily finished her sentence.

"I see the arrest record. For what it's worth, looks like he was provoked. Let me checked out the domestic violence. Hmm. He called the police on her as well. Several times."

"What's that mean?" She took a sip of her drink, wondering why it tasted so good when whenever she made tea it came out too weak.

Rebecca typed in more information. "They divorced eight years ago and there was a custody battle. I'm betting both sides were trying to tip the scales in their own favor. Sean Mercer won full custody, so I'm guessing his wife had some skeletons in her closet."

"Can you find anything else on him?"

"Hmm, look away…"

"Are you going on the dark web or something?" Rebecca laughed. "Not quite, but you're better off not knowing."

Emily listened to the quickening cadence of keys clicking under Rebecca's fingers. "Find anything?"

"Looks like our Mr. Mercer has a history of mental illness. He's on some heavy duty psychiatric drugs, and he was Baker acted twice."

"What's that mean?"

"Hospitalized against his will because he presented a danger to himself or others."

"Interesting. Henry went to talk to him. I'm worried."

"As long as he's on these meds he should be okay. Besides, the hospitalizations were some time ago."

Abby came in, placing her camera bag on the coffee table. "Hi, Emily. Sorry to hear about the accident."

"We're all going to be fine, thank God. Were you on a shoot?"

"Yeah. The historical society has me photographing a few sites they'd like to restore. Doubt it'll happen though. Money's scarce. Want to see?" She opened the bag and showed Emily the shots through the camera. "I have to process these, but it gives you an idea."

Emily felt like she was looking through the View Master she had as a kid. "This is the church in the square, Right?"

"Yes. To the left is an old Bingo Hall the city wants to demolish. I hear there was more than Bingo going on there. Gambling was a town pastime according to the woman from the historic society. And the next ones are of some business—a dairy farm, and two lumber mills. They are the original buildings from when the town was founded. The town got its name from the lumber businesses powered by Sugarbury Falls."

"I wonder how many people know this town once relied heavily on the lumber industry."

"Christmas trees, too. The lady from the historical society says their dream is to turn one of the mills into a living museum, with actors demonstrating how it was in the old days. It'd be a great side job for the college students looking to make extra money."

"Interesting. Henry's family owned or worked for a lumber mill."

"Say no more," said Rebecca. "What was the family name?"

"Fox. Try Theodore Fox."

"Got it. His father built the business. Passed it on to his son."

"That would have been Henry's grandfather. Henry's father was the first to go to college. He was a physician. He never mentioned being involved with the mill."

"It was sold to another family, but went out of business shortly afterward."

Emily finished her drink. "Thanks, both of you." She headed toward home, taking the long way around the lake.

Meanwhile, Henry pulled up in front of Sean Mercer's house. It was run down, in need of paint, and the lawn was overrun with weeds. He wasn't sure what he'd say, but was driven to confront him. How dare he try to kill him and his family. He knocked, waited, knocked again.

"What do ya' want?" A man a bit younger than Henry cracked the door open. "Go away."

"I just want to talk to you. I'm Dr. Fox."

"Wait a minute. I remember that name. You're that doctor who helped keep my son's killer on the street. Get outta here before I make you sorry you came."

"Stop threatening me and my family. I know you killed Damari and Dan Fischer, but it has to stop. Now." He pushed his way in through the cracked door.

"I'm gonna call the police. Not that they've been much help."

Henry smelled beer on Mercer's breath. "I'm not responsible for your son's death. It was an accident."

"The hell you're not. You told the court speed didn't kill my boy when I know that slime ball doctor was speeding. I was with my son that day. I saw it myself."

"His injuries were typical for an accident at normal speed. And was it worth killing Damari over?"

"Who?"

"The witness who testified Dan Fischer wasn't speeding."

"I didn't kill nobody. Not yet, at least." He picked up an umbrella from the stand near the door. "Looks like you didn't fare well in your last fight either." He whacked Henry with it, until Henry managed to grab it out of his hands and throw it across the room.

"This isn't the last you've heard from me. You're going to jail." He slammed the door behind him. On his way to the Audi, he saw something sticking out from behind the house and walked around. A canoe! And Mercer's car had a boat trailer behind it. He wondered if there were traces of blood in that canoe. Traces of Damari's blood.

Chapter 27

Henry stormed into the cabin. "Emily, he's guilty. I know it."

"You never should have gone over there alone. Are you okay? Did he admit to killing Damari and Dan?"

"No, but I saw a canoe in his yard and a trailer hooked to his white SUV. I'm going to call Megan."

Dallas, carrying his tool box, came in from the kitchen. "All done. There's some dust to clear but the cabinets look great. Come see."

Henry, too angry to care, plopped down on the sofa while Emily followed Dallas.

"This looks wonderful." She took out her phone. "Here's the before picture."

"Looks like a whole different house. Now we need an after."

Emily snapped a photo. "Let me get my checkbook. Be right back."

When she returned to the living room, Henry was talking to Megan on the phone.

"Yes, I'm sure. It has to be him. I bet you'll find blood in the canoe. And see if he's missing an oar while you're at it. No, I don't have anything tying him to Dan or my little encounter. Isn't that your job?" He hung up.

"Henry, don't be like that. They're on our side."

"When my family is threatened, It's urgent."

Emily wrote out a check and brought it to the kitchen. "Thanks a million, Dallas. Now go home and take your wife and baby out for a nice steak dinner. A new steak house opened near the Walmart last month. I don't eat meat, but I've heard raves about it."

"Maybe I'll give it a try. Alexandra loves steak and baked potatoes."

"Then she's a sophisticated eater for an infant. Watch out, she's going to be expensive to feed."

After he left, Emily cuddled on the couch next to Henry. "I saw Rebecca and Abby today. Rebecca found out Mercer has a history of mental illness. I hope you'll stay away from him from now on."

"He's a drunken buffoon if you ask me. I can picture him getting angry and hitting Damari with an oar. He came after me with an umbrella."

"Are you okay?"

"An umbrella, Emily. I'm fine."

"Abby was taking pictures for the historical society. She had a photo of the church in the square, a bingo hall, and a few abandoned farms and lumber mills. Did you know your great grandfather owned a lumber mill?"

"Yeah. My grandfather took it over after he died. They wanted my father to take the reins when Grandpa was ready to retire, but he had a different vision for himself."

"He wanted to become a doctor, right?"

"Yeah. Manual labor wasn't his thing and he hated the idea of running a business."

Henry's phone rang. "Megan, yeah, we're home. No, I didn't threaten him; in fact, he threatened me. He's our man, I'm sure of it. What email? Really? See, that proves it. Restraining order? I won't go near his place again but can't wait to visit him when he's behind bars."

"Henry, you will stay away, right?"

"Yeah. He's not going to admit anything. I'm hoping the police get a warrant and search that canoe of his. I'll bet there's physical evidence that will put him away."

"What email was Megan talking about?"

"It was from a woman who said she was on a date with Dan Fischer one night and Mercer came up to them and threatened Dan."

"Just now this comes up?"

"She thought it sounded fishy, too. She says they get all sorts of tips that never pan out in these kinds of cases." Perhaps *Nurse McPhee had an attack of conscious.*

"Should we call Maddy and say goodnight?" She reached in her pocket and on the coffee table. "I must have left it in the kitchen."

Henry turned on the TV while she was retrieving the phone and began channel surfing. He landed on a documentary about gambling in America.

"It was right on the table where I left it," said Emily. "What are you watching?"

"It's about the history of gambling. It was a big problem a hundred years ago, and it still is."

"Turn it up. That looks like the place Abby photographed. It's a bingo hall. Not the one in the square, but looks similar."

"It's a bingo hall that was a front for mob-run poker games. What a great cover. According to this show, it was pretty common." Henry went into the kitchen. "Want some coffee? I can put a pot on?"

"Sure. Didn't we see something in those newspaper clippings about gambling? I'm going to get the articles."

"I'll do it. You shouldn't be climbing up and down from the loft any more than you have to with one arm out of commission." He started the coffee, then went upstairs for the clippings.

Emily's eyes were glued to the TV. The show was talking about how illegal gambling was often signified by placing a playing card under the mat. Did the playing card in the silver box have something to do with gambling?

"Here you go. I got the articles and the old bible. Let's see here…" Henry read the headlines. "I'm not seeing much."

Emily flipped through the old bible. She found various papers stuck in between the pages. "Here's the original deed to the cabin. I thought he built it himself?"

"My grandfather made comments when I started puttering with woodworking. He said I got my talent from his father. But no one builds a house singlehandedly. He had to have had help." Henry stopped sifting. "This is an article about the disappearance of Charles Rivers. He was last seen near the town square, then seemed to vanish off the face of the earth."

"His family must have been worried sick."

"It doesn't mention him having a family." He read through more articles. "He was unmarried. Not surprising. He was unscrupulous. Stole businesses out from under people. Looks like he had a lot of enemies. Possible mob connections."

Emily said, "I think I found something. Look! It's a transfer of title. Your grandfather was transferring ownership of the lumber mill to Charles Rivers. What's the date of his disappearance?"

Henry looked back through the articles. "June 2, 1910."

"This contract was signed by Charles Rivers, on June 1. And it has your grandfather's signature as well."

"The mill technically belonged to Rivers at the time of his death."

"But it stayed in your family for another generation, right?"

"It wasn't sold until my father decided to go to college."

"Why was your grandfather transferring ownership of the mill, and how lucky was he that Charles Rivers went and disappeared before it could happen?"

"I'm not sure I want to connect these dots. Let's call Maddy and say goodnight. Enough investigating for today."

Emily picked up her phone. "Maddy, how are you feeling? That's good. Who's there with you?" She whispered to Henry, "It's Robby."

"Let me say goodnight." He took the phone. "Hi, honey. Yes, I'm thrilled Robby is out and it's so nice he's keeping you company. We'll be by in the morning. Love you."

"She sounded very upbeat. Do you think Robby is the reason? Are they becoming more than friends?"

"I'm not sure I'm ready for it if they are. This is a whole new phase. Where did you put those parenting manuals?"

Chapter 28

In the morning, Emily and Henry headed to the hospital to see Maddy. When they got to her room, she was sipping juice and picking at a plate of scrambled eggs.

"I see you've graduated to real food," said Emily.

"If you can call it that. These are pretty awful."

Henry said, "But it's a sign of progress. Your doctor says you're healing nicely and can come home in a few days."

"Wait till you see the kitchen! How was your visit with Robby?" asked Emily.

"He's so sweet. We talked for hours. We have so much in common. Coralee said he can stay at the inn rent free if he picks up some odd jobs for her. She says the fall foliage season is coming up and there are a lot of little repairs to be done."

"I thought Dallas was handling those? And Noah? And Franklin?" said Henry.

"You know Coralee," said Emily. "She always finds a way to help others. Besides, Dallas will be going back to his teaching job soon and Noah has school in the fall."

"And Robby? Isn't he going back to school?"

"Of course. Robby said after seeing Jonathan in action, he wants to be a lawyer. He's really smart, you know. And he needs the money."

"I can tell by talking to him that he's smart," said Emily. "It's just that he's quite a few years older than you, Maddy."

"But I feel like I've known him forever."

Emily gave Henry a knowing look. Between the two of them watching Robby like a hawk, Maddy would be protected. Overprotected.

Henry received a text. "Chauncey has turned a corner. Looks like he's going to make it. Come on, let's stop by his room." He and Emily kissed Maddy and took the elevator to Chauncey's floor.

"If he can identify the car that hit him as Mercer's, we've got him," said Henry.

On the way to his room, they ran into Megan.

"Did he give a statement? Mercer's guilty, right?"

Megan sighed. "Unfortunately, Chauncey's memory is sketchy right now. The doctor said that's normal."

"Yeah, but maybe you can show him a picture of Mercer's car. That'll jog his memory."

"His doctor said to let him rest and try again later. We don't want him to regress. Besides, his wife is in there with him. I'd keep it short if I were you."

"What about the blood on the oar?"

"We're working on it. At least Robby is home now. If Mercer's the one, we'll get him. Trust me."

Henry and Emily walked into Chauncey's room, which again smelled of lavender. His wife was holding his hand and catching him up on all the news that he'd missed.

"I'm so glad he's turned the corner," said Emily. "How are you feeling, Chauncey?"

His wife held up a cup and brought the straw to his lips. His voice was raspy and it seemed to be an effort to speak.

"I feel like I've been run over by a truck!" He started to laugh, then started coughing. His wife gave him more water.

"The detective says you can't remember what the truck looked like."

"My head is so fuzzy. I ain't thinking straight."

Henry pressed on. "Do you remember a guy named Sean Mercer? His son was killed in a snowmobile accident. Dan Fisher stood trial for causing the accident, but he was acquitted."

"Sort of remember."

"Did you treat the Mercer boy when he arrived at the hospital? Or did you give a statement?"

"No, I don't think so. Why?"

The police think Mercer may be responsible for both Damari Cooper and Dan Fischer's deaths."

His wife said, "That was last winter, right? We'd gone to visit my sister over the holidays and heard about it when we got back. Chauncey wasn't even here."

"Are you sure?"

"Course I'm sure. I'm not the one with a head injury." She looked at her husband. "My Chauncey's real tired. He needs to sleep now."

"Of course. Good to see you're doing better. Get some rest. Doctor's orders."

Henry closed the door softly behind them.

"That's a dead end," said Emily.

"Not necessarily. I want to hear it from Chauncey himself when he's feeling better. I know the three attacks are related."

"Four," said Emily. "You mean four." She pointed to his eye and patted her cast.

"Let me drop you off at home. I'm supposed to put in a couple of hours this afternoon."

On the way home, Emily suggested finding out more about Henry's grandfather and the missing Charles Rivers. "Why don't we stop by Rebecca and Abby's on the way?" She called ahead and Rebecca said she'd found some news.

"Okay, but I can't stay long."

Henry knocked and immediately heard Milo bark. "That's what we need. A dog for protection."

"Try telling that to Chester."

Rebecca came to the door in basketball shorts and a Yale t-shirt. "How's Maddy doing?"

"Much better. She should be home in a few days," said Emily.

"Come, see what I found." She opened her laptop. "Charles Rivers had lots of enemies. One theory is that he ran off with investor's money to some tropical island, escaping the lawsuits piling up against him. He'd drained his bank account the day he disappeared, over a million dollars. Back then, imagine how much money that was."

"So he fled before he got arrested and had to pay back his investors. But why did he leave the lumber mill? We found a contract in with Henry's grandfather's things. The contract transferring ownership was dated the day before he disappeared."

"And the money was never recovered, I assume."

"Nope. He also owed lots of back taxes. And he had gambling debts. Maybe it was worth it to cut his losses and leave the mill behind."

"Wasn't murder a theory?"

"Yeah, they looked into several leads, but the body was never found, and there were witnesses who thought they saw him at the train station, the airport, the general store…you get the picture."

"Eyewitness reports are notoriously flawed," said Emily. "I'm going to spend the afternoon going through the papers and bible we found once again."

"From what I'm seeing, I'm not entirely convinced he left on his own," said Rebecca. "It said in one of the articles he had a treasured baseball card collection worth a ton of money. Had a Ty Cobb card and Cy Young, too."

"And he left it behind?"

"Weird, right? He could have tucked them into his pocket. Why leave them behind? And there's a police report I accessed which says they found a shoe on a road heading out of town. They think it may have belonged to Rivers."

"If he was murdered, what happened to the body? Did they check the rivers and lakes?"

"Yeah. And sent dogs into the woods looking. Nothing turned up. Believe me, all those cheated investors and gamblers he owed—I'm sure they left no stone unturned."

"Thanks, Rebecca. We appreciate the info."

When they got back to the house, Emily sat with the things they'd found in the crawl space. Why did Theodore Fox keep those articles about Rivers? And why was his involvement with Rivers important enough for Henry's grandfather to include in the silly clue box? She sifted through the box.

"Em, I'm going back to the hospital. See you at dinner."

"Okay." She leafed through the family bible. It wasn't closing right. It had been sitting there for a long time, but yesterday she hadn't noticed it. She put on her reading glasses, which she should have been using all along rather than straining her eyes. Something about the spine didn't feel right. After working her fingers into the binding, she made a discovery. A gold chain with the letter *C*. And it was covered with something. Something that looked a lot like dried blood.

Chapter 29

Emily sorted through the newspaper clippings for pictures of Charles Rivers. Scrutinizing each one, she found the confirmation she needed. In one of the photos, Charles Rivers wore the gold chain with the letter *C* hanging from it.

She tried Henry, but his phone went to voicemail. What if Theodore Fox killed Charles Rivers? He had a great motive—keeping the family business. The *C* on the necklace stood for Charles. She planned to bring it right over to the police station. Where would he have buried the body?

She called Rebecca. "Where exactly was the shoe found? The one they thought belonged to Rivers?"

"On Mill Road heading out of town."

"Thanks, Rebecca."

She'd barely hung up when Maddy called.

"Emily? Robby is here and we just solved the anagram riddle. Robby found the word *mill*, so we played around with the letters and used the internet to search names of local saw mills and lumber mills. We think it says Tedgar Mill, which is just outside of town on Mill Road."

"Mill Road? That's where they found one of Charles River's shoes. I'll check and see if that was the name of the family mill. Good work. Rebecca will be proud."

She tried Henry again. "Hey, look. What was the name of the family lumber mill?"

"Not sure. I think my grandfather said the mill was started by his father and his father's best friend."

"Does Tedgar Mill sound familiar?"

"They called my grandfather Ted."

"And did he have a friend who started with Gar? Gariboldi? Gary?"

"I don't know. It could be Gary. Oops, I've got to go. They just brought in a new patient. Love ya."

Emily headed back to the papers and bible. She looked at a handful of photos, some labeled on the back. She could see the resemblance between Henry and Ted Fox. Henry's father as a little boy looked just like Henry when he was small. She put aside a picture of Henry with his grandfather that she thought he'd like to have. *Here's a picture in front of what looks like a mill.* She turned it over. *Ted and Gary opening day.* That was it. Now, what did Henry's grandfather want him to do with that information? Were the clues just leading Henry to finding out his grandfather was a murderer?

Chester swatted something shiny under the bed. The chain! She'd left it on the dresser. Extricating it from under Chester's paw, she wrapped it in a handkerchief and stuck it in her pocket. She had forgotten she'd meant to drop it off at the police station.

She grabbed her keys, went to the driveway, and realized Henry had her car! Now what? It wasn't like Sugarbury Falls had Uber, so she had to think. Rebecca and Abby? They both worked from home.

She started toward their cabin and after a few steps, noticed something on the ground. A wallet. She opened the worn leather wallet and pulled out a driver's license. Dallas Peterkin. How did he not notice he'd dropped this? Then again, with a new baby at home...she knew how she felt when she didn't get enough sleep. Maybe one of the girls wouldn't mind swinging by his cabin after the station so she could return it.

She knocked on the girls' door. No answer. Then she peeked in through the front window with the shade partially down. The room was dark, but Rebecca was using a black light to examine something. She was writing notes on a small dry erase board and was wearing earphones. She knocked louder and watched Rebecca hide the light and turn over the board before answering the door.

"Hey, Emily."

"Looks like you were busy. May I ask?"

"It's on a need to know basis, so better to forget you saw anything," said Rebecca. "You're not in danger, I swear." Rebecca laughed.

"I need your help if you're available. Remember Charles Rivers? I found a chain hidden in the family bible that I'm sure belongs to him." She pulled the handkerchief out of her pocket and unwrapped it. "I think that's dried blood. I want to bring it to the police station to have them check it out, but we're down to one car, which Henry has at the moment."

"I can tell you right now if it's blood." She pulled the shade down all the way, then opened her desk drawer and pulled out a spray bottle. She placed the chain on the desk, sprayed it, and turned out the lights so the interior of the cabin was pitch dark. "Yep. Look, it's glowing. It's blood all right." She flicked the lights back on.

"You're just full of surprises, Rebecca. Should I still bring it to the station?"

"Sure. They've got all sorts of new-fangled DNA testing they can do now."

"And here's another thing. I found our handyman's wallet. Can we drop it off on the way back?"

"Sure."

After swinging by the station, Emily got Dallas's address from Coralee. She half expected to find Dallas at the inn doing handy work, but Coralee had given him the day off. They followed the dirt road leading toward the lake and found the address.

"I don't think he's home," said Emily. "I don't see his van and the lights are off."

"Try the door. Around here, I've noticed no one locks their doors, which is crazy. We can leave it there with a note."

Emily tried the door and sure enough, it was unlocked. Neither his wife nor the baby were at home either. She moved the single stained placemat over and wrote a note to leave on top of the wallet. "Rebecca, what are you doing?"

Rebecca closed the refrigerator door. "Can't help it. Snooping's in my blood."

"Hopefully he took time to enjoy this place with his wife and baby. Seems like all he was doing was working all summer."

"Wife and baby? Look around. No highchair or bouncy seat. No bottles in the fridge." She opened the kitchen cabinets. "No formula or baby food."

Emily took a good look. "There's only one coffee mug in the sink."

"And the fridge consisted of a six pack of beer and a half eaten pack of hotdogs. What woman do you know who'd be living on hotdogs and beer?"

"Do you think we're in the right place?"

Rebecca picked up a stack of forwarded mail from the coffee table. "Dallas Peterkin, right?"

"Yes."

"We're in the right place. Whatever this guy told you about having a wife and baby is a big lie. That's my professional opinion."

Other things Dallas said over the course of the summer didn't add up now that she thought about it. She didn't know a lot about babies, but could infants really eat steak and potatoes? And play dress up? Why hadn't he shown off his new daughter, or at least shown pictures?

"Can you…"

"Do some digging? Of course. Let's go. Abby will be home soon and we have plans."

On the way back, Henry called. "Chauncey remembers the car that hit him. It was a white van, not a white SUV."

"White van?" Dallas Peterkin drove a white van. Maybe she was being overly suspicious because of what Rebecca just told her. Then again, she'd met Dallas's pregnant wife last summer. If she wasn't with him, where was she? Maybe they split up and she took off with the baby. He could be embarrassed to admit that.

"Emily, are you there?"

"Yes. Rebecca is driving me home. I have some news about Charles Rivers to share with you when you get home."

"Great. We'll catch up then."

Chapter 30

"I'm glad you suggested going out for dinner," said Emily. I was in no mood to cook."

"And you wanted to pump Coralee for info on Dallas Peterkin, right?"

"Why would he lie about having a wife and child?"

"He didn't lie. Last summer, I treated his pregnant wife. She fell and injured her head. It was just a concussion. You met her yourself."

"I did. And the baby was fine?"

"Yeah. Dan checked her out and gave them both a clean bill of health."

Given the beautiful weather and the early time, the dining room was emptier than usual. Coralee came over and set a basket of warm blueberry muffins on the table. "How's Maddy doing?"

Henry said, "Much better. She'll be home in a few days. What do you think of that Robby? We suspect there's a relationship starting between him and Maddy."

"He's quite a bit older than her," said Emily.

"That boy's got a heart of gold. You should see him around the cats! And he's patient, too. I saw him out on the porch a few times talking to 'the lumberjack,' you know, that old retiree who hangs out here playing chess with the guests."

"If he has the wear-with-all to spend more than five minutes with that old bag of wind, he's definitely patient," said Emily.

"In the scheme of things, he's not that much older, what, 5 or 6 years? My Travis, may he rest in peace, was ten years older than me and it worked out just fine. He was the love of my life."

"Speak of the devil," said Henry. "Isn't that the lumberjack out there in the lobby?"

"Henry, I have an idea. Do you think he knows anything about your family's business? He's probably as old as your grandfather would have been."

"Not quite, but they may have crossed paths."

Coralee said, "Are you still digging up info on those clues your family left? He'd be a good one to talk to. Let me bring him in."

Before they could object, Coralee was out in the lobby.

"So much for a relaxing dinner," said Henry.

"Who knows, maybe he can help piece together your family puzzle. If he drones on too long, we'll pretend Maddy has an emergency."

"And leave our dinner sitting here?"

"We'll take it to go."

Coralee led a burly, hunchbacked man with a long Santa Claus beard to the table and pulled over a chair for him. "What can I get you for dinner?"

"Vegetarian chili for me," said Emily. "With the house salad."

Henry ordered pot pie. The lumberjack ordered two.

Emily explained the clues found in the silver box as well as what they'd found in the family bible and crates from the crawl space.

"I knew your grandfather, Henry. I was little, but I shadowed my father whenever I was off school. Got to know the guys. Pops worked at your Grandfather's mill."

"The Tedgar mill, right?"

"Yeah, but it was more Ted than Gar. Old Gary lost his arm at the mill and became a partner mostly in name after that. Ted Fox was one hard worker. Always at the mill except for when he was at the gambling hall. My mother used to get on my father about that all the time. Bingo Hall was a front for high stakes poker games."

"And you remember that all these years later?"

"Only because my parents constantly fought about it. Dad defended it by listing the others who he played Poker with—Ted Fox, Old Gary, and Charlie Rivers."

Henry leaned in closer. "What do you know about Charlie Rivers?"

"You heard the stories, I'm sure. Disappeared without a trace. Some say he ran off with stolen money from his investors. Some called it murder, but they never found the body. Or the money."

"Could Henry's grandfather have been involved somehow with the disappearance?"

"Couldn't tell ya'. My father was one of the last to see him though. He saw him at the poker game where he pulled out a royal flush, and the next day he was reported missing."

"You remember that from so long ago?"

"My long term memory's clear as a bell. Now ask me what I ate for breakfast and it's another story."

"Do you remember anything else?"

"I heard my father saying he lost a boat load of money that night. They all did, except for Charlie. Dad was going to have to sell a tractor to pay off his debt. He was relieved when Charlie went missing."

"So it's possible my grandfather lost money as well."

"Where there's a winner there are losers."

Coralee came back to the table. "That guest you were playing chess with yesterday is out on the porch asking for you."

The lumberjack stood up. "Can't pass up a chess match now, can I?"

When he'd slowly made his way out of the dining room, Emily said, "Coralee, there's something I want to ask you about. Some things about Dallas Peterkin aren't adding up. I went by his cabin to return something he left and there was no sign of a wife or baby."

"Really? I haven't seen his wife all summer, but he said she liked to keep the baby sheltered from germs so she didn't want to be out in public."

"Why wouldn't he at least be showing off pictures?"

"Don't know. Maybe he and his wife are on the outs. The stress of a baby has broken up more than one couple I've known. He could just be embarrassed to admit they aren't with him."

"Yeah, that crossed my mind, too." Her phone vibrated. "It's the police station." She went out on the porch to take the call.

Coralee said to Henry, "I knew all along Robby was innocent, but do the police have any other suspects?"

"Not at the moment. We're still trying to tie together Damari, Dan, and Chauncey. What did they have in common that made them a target?"

He left out the part about Dan's warning, and the probable motive for his brakes being tampered with. Emily returned.

"That was Megan. The gold chain did have blood on it. She's sending it to Burlington for DNA testing. I'll bet it belonged to Charlie Rivers."

Coralee said, "You think Henry's grandfather left clues because he killed Charlie Rivers? Why would he do that?"

Henry said, "There was a boatload of money that went missing along with Charlie Rivers. I'm wondering if grandfather hid it somewhere. He couldn't very well deposit it into his bank account."

"And if the whole Charlie Rivers thing had time to be forgotten…"

"His descendants could enjoy it," said Coralee. "Did you check the family mill out on Mill Road? It's all abandoned and overgrown now, but what a great hiding place. Plus, all the wood chippers and all…"

"Coralee!"

"Sorry, I've been reading too many spy novels lately."

"She may have a point," said Henry. "There is a skeleton key in the box. Something's hidden somewhere. And don't forget the card. Rivers and my grandfather both played poker, and the lumberjack just told us everyone lost money the night before Rivers was discovered missing."

Coralee said, "Looks like this town's got two mysteries to solve. Emily, you may have your next true crime book in your pocket!"

Chapter 31

"I knew you were going to suggest this," said Henry. "As soon as the lumberjack started in on the gambling and the old mill, I figured you'd want to drive out there."

"You're off today, and Maddy comes home tomorrow. Let's take advantage of the opportunity."

Emily replenished Chester's cat food, having learned to manipulate the bag using one arm. Amazing how adaptable one could be when necessary. Too bad she wasn't typing her book a little faster with her one good hand. She threw on a pair of denim shorts and a baggy t-shirt, which easily fit over her cast.

"So the mill first, or the cemetery?"

"The mill."

Henry opened the passenger door for Emily. "Maddy's going to be mad we didn't wait for her."

"I know, but her stomach is still tender from the surgery. She shouldn't be traipsing around the mill. What if she was to fall on the stitches?"

"You have a point." He started the car. "What are you expecting to find at the mill?"

"Hate to say it, but maybe a body, or I guess I should say skeleton."

"After my grandfather sold the mill, the new owner didn't report anything, so if there's a body there, it must be well hidden." He zipped down the road wondering if he should consider another Audi if the Tesla thing didn't work out. The mill was further than he'd anticipated. He pulled onto what had once been a dirt path, but now was a jungle of weeds. Only the taller weeds flanking it hinted that it was ever a road.

"Henry, there's a sign. I can barely read it."

"Jinson's Mill. Boy it looks like a ghost town out here." He trudged through the weeds until the once path disappeared. "Looks like we're on foot from here on."

He helped Emily out and they walked toward the mill. Debris cluttered the place and he kicked what he could aside to clear the course. Emily grabbed his arm, nearly losing her balance on several occasions. She heard, or hopefully just imagined, rustling in the grass. *It's just the wind, not a snake.* Even in broad daylight, her fight or flight hormones kicked into high gear.

It was slow going, but finally they made it to the wooden building and abandoned machinery. "Most of this is rusted through," said Emily. "Jinson should have sold this stuff instead of leaving it to rot."

Henry ran his hand over rusty metal. "I think they fed the logs in here and the saw cut them into boards…and no. It's too small to fit a body through."

"What's this?"

"An industrial sander."

They walked along the length of the machinery and out the back. Henry swatted at the black flies buzzing in his ear. "I don't know where to start. The mill is surrounded by these woods. He could have easily hidden a body out there, too."

"Let's think about the clues. Maybe we're missing something." She ran through what she could remember of Gray's *Elegy*, pictured the playing card, river, chimes…

"Let's keep walking," said Henry. He cleared the path around the back of the mill with his feet, stopping periodically to move aside larger branches.

"Wait! Do you hear that?" Emily grabbed his arm.

"What?"

"Listen." The wind had picked up as the afternoon clouds rolled in. "Chimes. I hear wind chimes."

Emily led the way. "See? Over there by that barn or whatever it is."

"Some sort of storage shed. Next to a bubbling brook, like in the poem!" She looked up. "They're tied to that tree."

They hustled over to the tree. Emily scraped her hand on the bark and without missing a beat, wiped the dirt and blood on her shorts. When she reached the back of the tree, she noticed something carved deeply into the bark.

"Henry! Come quick! Look!"

"What is it?" He worked his way around the tree. "You're kidding."

"It's an ace of spades. Someone even took the trouble of painting it. Isn't an ace part of a royal flush?"

"It has to be a clue."

"Start digging."

"Emily, there's no way we can do this ourselves."

"There's all sorts of tools laying around."

"It has to be done carefully. If there are bones under there, we don't want to break or miss them." He took out his phone. "I'm calling Megan to tell her what we found. I'll bet the police have the resources to dig this up."

While he called, Emily wondered how long it would take before the area could be dug up. What if the body was here under the tree? Or maybe the money was hidden here.

"Megan's sending a crew out this afternoon. We might as well go home."

"Are you kidding? And miss the big reveal?"

"It may be hours if not longer."

Emily sighed, "Guess you're right." She offered a compromise. "Let's stop at the cemetery."

Knowing he wouldn't win, and curious himself, Henry led them back to the silver Audi, which was now sprinkled like an ice cream cone with leaves and dirt courtesy of the pre-storm winds. Now that he had his bearings, he took a shorter route home. On the way, they passed a cornfield with a bunch of cars parked at its edge.

"I think that's the new corn maze that opened this summer. We should do it with Maddy when she gets better. We could bring Robby, too."

"Looks like fun. What happens if we get lost?"

"I think they use GPS embedded along the way. You and Maddy are good with puzzles."

"Says the true crime writer turned amateur sleuth!"

He pulled in front of the old church. "You can't possibly hop the fence with that arm. I should have considered that before agreeing to stop here."

Disappointed that she couldn't see a way around it, she said, "Then you go and take a look around."

Henry worked his way over the iron gate, jumping to the other side. He headed to his grandfather's grave and cleared away the debris around the base of the tombstone. He couldn't have hidden the money here if he was already dead. Didn't make sense. He looked around at the neighboring stones. He wiped off the dirt on the closest headstone. They had already cleared the neighboring tombstones on one side. *What about the other side?* He picked up a flat rock to scrape away the dirt covering the inscription.

*Mary Fox. 1910-1968.* His grandmother. He'd gone to her funeral as a child. Was this the same church? He remembered his mother holding his hand, and his father crying. It was the first and last time he'd seen his father cry.

He cleared away the branches and beside the headstone, uncovered a smaller one between the two graves. It was a flat piece of granite inscribed *Patience Fox. 1965-1965*. It made no sense. He never heard of Patience Fox, and apparently she died as an infant, or even during childbirth. His grandparents were the same age. That meant his grandmother would have given birth when she was 55 years old. Emily's age. No way. He inspected the stone more closely. The *T* in Patience was ornate, maybe it was supposed to resemble a cross.

"Henry, come on. Did you find something?"

He brushed off his legs and went back to the gate. "I may have found a dead relative." He climbed the fence and hopped down. "Patience Fox. Died as an infant."

"Patience? Sounds like a Quaker name."

"My family was Presbyterian. So is this whole church/graveyard set up."

"When we get home, I'll check the family bible and see if it lists her."

Chapter 32

When they got home, Emily flicked on the lights and made a beeline for the bible.

"I don't see a Patience Fox listed anywhere. It looks like your grandmother kept meticulous notes. If she had a baby, there'd be a birth certificate or something."

Henry's phone rang. His heart skipped a beat. The police digging crew had to have found something by now. What if they didn't and this was all a disappointing waste of time? He hit the accept button.

"Yes, Megan. No way!" Emily pulled at his sleeve and motioned for him to hit speaker, but he ignored her. "Can you identify it? Is it Charlie Rivers? Yeah. Thanks."

"They found a body, right?"

"A skeleton, right under the chimes."

"Is it him?"

"They have to test it. Megan's hoping there are dental records. Says that'd be the quickest way to identify it."

"Let's assume your grandfather killed Rivers and buried him under the chimes. Did they find the money, too?"

"She didn't mention it."

"So he killed Rivers, took back the deed and the money Rivers won at the poker game. Where's the money? Burying it would have made sense."

"It would. Maybe he did bury it, just not with the body."

"What do you mean?"

"*Patience Fox.* What if he meant *Patience, Fox.*? Maybe the money is buried in the cemetery! The headstone was a flat piece of granite on the ground, not sticking up like the others."

Emily retrieved the silver box and the clues. "The chimes were where he buried the body. Rivers was the name of the victim. The playing card is an ace of spades, assumedly part of the winning royal flush poker hand. Gray's *Elegy*, is of course, the graveyard. What about the key? That's the only clue we haven't used."

Henry picked up the key and examined it from different angels. Then he brought it under the lamp and put on his reading glasses. "Emily, the *t* in *Patience* is different. It's ornate, not like the other letters. I thought it was supposed to be a cross, but maybe..."

"Maybe it's supposed to be the key! I'll bet if we go back there, we'll find a way to use the key to get the money. Come on."

"Emily, it'll be getting dark soon."

She was afraid he'd say they should wait until the morning, but instead, he said, "I'll grab a shovel and some flashlights."

Henry pushed the speed limit going back to the cemetery. He knew he needed Emily's help, but worried about her climbing the fence with her broken arm.

As if reading his mind, Emily said, "If you go over first, you can help me down. I'll be careful. I can still grip kind of with my left hand."

When they arrived, Henry had her try to grip the bar on the fence. "It's tough, but I can do it."

He tossed the shovel and flashlights over, then hopped down himself. "Come on, very slowly. Put your weight on your right side."

She struggled, and lost her grip when she swung her legs over the top.

"I've got you." Henry caught her and set her safely down. "Let's go." He led her to the flat stone, brushing off the bit of dirt that had blown over it in the last few hours. He dug his fingers around the edges. "Hand me the shovel."

He stood up and managed to pry the shovel under the edge of the stone.

Emily cringed as she listened to the shovel scraping against the edge of the stone like nails on a chalk board. "Have you got it? It looks like it's moving."

"Almost." He loosened the ground around the edges and used the shovel as a lever. Putting all his weight on the handle, he heard a pop. The grave separated from the ground.

"You did it!" She bent down and helped pull off the stone, which wasn't as thick as it had appeared.

Working together, they cleared the area under the stone. Henry shoveled. He hoped his Fitbit was getting all this. Sweat dripped from his forehead.

"It's getting dark. Need the light?" She held it over the area.

"I think I hit something." He shoveled faster.

"I hope it isn't a coffin."

"It's too shallow to have buried a coffin." Fighting growing fatigue and the ache in his arms, he worked as quickly as possible. "I've got it."

He lifted out a small, metal box with a padlock. "Where's that key?"

Emily handed him the key from her pocket which he jiggled into the lock. When she heard a click, she screamed. "It's open!"

Henry grabbed the flashlight. "I think we've just found ourselves some buried treasure."

Emily lifted stacks of money out of the box. "Let's get this home."

It was difficult to sleep. In the morning, Megan called.

"Dental records confirm the skeleton is Charlie Rivers. Even has an intact gold crown on one of the molars."

Henry said, "So my grandfather was a murderer. Nothing like a bit of a smear on the old family history. Oh, and we found the money. It was buried in the cemetery. What should we do with it? Does Rivers have living relatives?"

"No living relatives popped up in our search. Finders keepers. Put it to good use." He stuck the phone in his pocket.

"She says we can keep the money. Put it to good use."

"I can't wait to pick up Maddy and tell her we've solved the puzzle. She can help us decide how to use the money."

When they arrived at the hospital, they passed Chauncey being wheeled out the front door alongside his wife, who was holding a plant and a balloon bouquet.

"Chauncey, they finally sprung you," said Henry.

"I can't wait to sleep in my own bed, eat my wife's home cookin', and catch up on Netflix. I've got a few weeks before I have to come back to work."

"We've missed you."

"You know, I've been getting back pieces of my memory. I'm positive it was a white van that hit me. It had a New York plate on the front. Never got to see the back."

"That's great. I hope you told the police."

"I sure did."

His wife said, "I'm not stopping till they find that idiot who hit my Chauncey."

"I'm sure they will," said Emily.

"Enough with the bad. Here's some good news. Guess what? We just found out we're having a baby."

"Congratulations," said Emily. She gave them both a hug.

"A baby. What a highlight after that setback."

"It ain't but the size of a pea and already it's our whole life. All I want to do is protect him."

"Or her," said his wife. Sometimes I wake up at night and worry that with all this stress, I'm going to lose her. When I heard that heartbeat, can't tell you how that felt. If anything happens I'll go crazy."

Henry said, "Once you've heard the heartbeat, chances are it will turn out just fine. And once you're past the first trimester, it'd take some bad injury or a genetic glitch to stop it from being born."

"Best of luck to you both," said Emily. "We've got a shelf full of parenting books if you need to borrow them."

They continued into the hospital to Maddy's room, where Robby was waiting with her. She was sitting on the edge of the bed, dressed in loose jeans and the *no fracking* t-shirt Robby wore the first time Emily saw him.

"Ready to blow this pop stand?" asked Henry.

"Huh?"

Emily shook her head at her husband. "He means, are you ready to go home? Chester missed you. He sleeps on your bed all day long."

"Can Robby come over?"

"Why don't we get you settled in and he can come by later for dinner."

In the car, they told Maddy about the money and finding Charlie Rivers.

"That's unbelievable. Wow. What are you going to do with the money?"

Henry said, "We'll think of something. After the evil way it was acquired, I want to do some good with it."

"One mystery solved, one to go," said Emily.

Chapter 33

Maddy kissed Chester, then opened her laptop.

"Emily, Henry, look. It's from that girl, Feo. She says thank you to whoever sent help her way. Knowing someone cared made all the difference. And she signed it Briana. Not Feo."

"I'm proud of you for reaching out to her. It would have been so easy to ignore the message and who knows what she would have done."

Henry said, "We never know what our little ripples affect. As a doctor, I remind myself of that often. I'm proud of you, too."

Shortly after arriving home, Megan called.

"We ran tests on Mercer's car and there's no evidence at all he ran over Chauncey or caused Dan's death."

"Did you search his house for traces of brake fluid?" said Henry.

"He cooperated. Had nothing to hide. There weren't any tools lying around that he could have used to sabotage your brakes. His garage was virtually empty. Also, Chauncey says the van had New York plates, which Mercer's SUV doesn't."

Emily tugged at him. "Ask her about the oar."

"Did you find blood on the oar at his house?"

"No, and the size didn't match up with Damari's bruise. He's not our man."

"If it's not Mercer, who is it? We've crossed everyone off the suspect list." He heard a knock. "Someone's at the door. Keep me posted."

Emily answered the door. "Hi, Rebecca. Did you find something?"

"Sure did. I did some digging. I searched and searched and guess what I found?"

Henry wished she'd lose the drama and just get to the point already.

"I found a death certificate for Lisa Peterkin and another for an Alexandra Peterkin. They both died on the same day last October."

Emily's jaw dropped to the floor. Now it all made sense. She thought about what Chauncey's wife's words echoed in her head. *I'd do anything to protect my baby. I'd go crazy if something happened to it.*

"Henry, you said you saw Lisa Peterkin after the fall she took last summer. Was there any kind of injury?"

"Just a minor concussion. Dan checked her over and the baby was fine."

"Who else tended to her?"

"Chauncey practically lived in the ER last summer since we were short-handed. Chances are he did."

"Damari worked there too, right?" said Emily.

"Yeah. As a matter of fact, she'd just started around that time."

"What if his wife and baby died and Dallas blamed the four of you?"

"But she didn't die. They were both fine when they went back home at the end of the summer." The light bulb went on. *Was there a complication later? After they went back home?* "I'm going to run over to the hospital and see what I can piece together."

"I'm coming too. Maddy, will you be all right by yourself?"

"Yeah. Robby will be here soon."

On the way to the hospital, Henry called Chauncey.

"Hate to bother you so soon after coming home, but do you remember treating a Lisa Peterkin? She was pregnant, fell, had a concussion? Yes, last summer. That's right. Do you remember if Damari was working reception then? Okay. Thanks. Get some rest."

Emily said, "Did he remember?"

"Yes, he was one of her nurses. And he's sure Damari was there because she worked the day shift all summer, even weekends."

"I just thought of something. Dallas was in and out of Coralee's all summer doing repairs. He would have had access to Robby's room. I'll bet *he* framed Robby."

"You're probably right. I want to check my records and see if I missed something when I treated his wife." He pulled into the hospital parking lot and put on his ID badge. "Let's go."

He and Emily headed to his office. Waiting for the computer to boot up, Emily drummed her fingers on his desk.

"Here we go." Henry pulled up the records. "She left here with a clean bill of health. I'm going to call her doctor."

He looked up the number and made the call. "This is Dr. Fox from Vermont. I need to speak to him regarding a patient. Tell him it's urgent." He exhaled audibly. "Yes, I'll hold." Now it was his turn to drum his fingers on the desk.

"What's taking so long?" said Emily.

"She's getting him. At least he's in the office." He put the phone on speaker. "She's transferring me."

"This is Dr. Wallace. How can I help you?"

"I'm Dr. Henry Fox from Vermont. It's about a patient. Lisa Peterkin. Mrs. Peterkin was visiting and in the middle trimester of pregnancy when she had a fall here last summer. Minor concussion. Our ob-gyn looked her over as well. His notes say the baby had a strong heartbeat. The ultra sound in her file looks normal. I understand she and the baby passed away last

October and was hoping you could provide information as to what occurred."

"Give me a minute to access her file."

Henry drummed his fingers on the desk. *Doesn't she have a computer? What's taking so long?*

Dr. Wallace came back on the line. "Mrs. Peterkin died of an aneurysm. The fetus died along with her."

"Was the aneurysm related to the head injury?"

"It's unlikely but not unheard of. I remember her now. Her husband blamed anyone and everyone for negligence. Tried to go after me for it."

"He attacked you?"

"No, of course not. He hired himself a lawyer who did his homework and told him he didn't have a case."

"Thank you for your help. Much appreciated." He turned to Emily. "There you have it."

"Dallas blames you and Dr. Fischer for missing the aneurysm."

"And Damari, probably for not getting her into treatment quickly enough. They triage the patients, but remember Damari had just started working and it took her a while to develop efficiency."

"And Chauncey was her nurse. Dallas thought he should have picked up on it, right?"

"I'll call Megan." He had the phone in his hand, when Emily's rang.

"Henry, I think this number is Dallas."

"How'd he have your number?"

"I gave it to him when he was working on the kitchen." She pressed the button. "Hello. Yes." She started shaking. "Okay, we'll be there. No police. You better not hurt her. She just got out of the hospital."

Henry said, "Tell me!"

"He's got Maddy. We're supposed to meet him at the corn maze. He wants to talk to you."

"I'm calling the police."

"No! He said he'd kill her if we brought the cops."

Henry turned off the computer and grabbed Emily's hand. By the time they got back to the car, the sun had gone down. Henry flew over the roads, barely breathing until they were parked at the maze.

"No one's here. The sign says they close at 5:00."

"Look over behind the ticket booth. It's Dallas's van."

Emily shouted his name. "Dallas, we're here. Alone, no cops. You said you wanted to talk to Henry. He's right here."

The only sound was the chirping of crickets. "I'm here. I didn't kill your wife or your baby. Even your lawyer told you that. Come on, you coward. Come out where I can see you, man to man."

A voice came over a megaphone. "How does it feel to have your daughter in jeopardy? To know her life may end at any moment?"

Emily cried. "Dallas, no. She's an innocent young girl. She didn't do anything to you."

"And my baby wasn't innocent? She didn't even get to take her first breath thanks to your husband." The voice had drifted away from the stand and she and Henry followed it.

"Dr. Fox. You're supposed to heal people not kill them."

"I treated your wife for a concussion. I didn't kill her."

"You didn't save her. She had an aneurysm. Never heard of it? That's what they call it when a blood vessel swells up and bursts."

Henry and Emily followed the voice and were now well into the corn maze. "Aneurysms are rarely associated with brain injuries. Less than one percent are related to a traumatic injury."

"Stop with your messed up doctor talk. You should have noticed it. So should that Dr. Fischer, the baby doctor. He missed it and killed Alexandra."

"There was no way to know."

"And that fat, black nurse. Lisa kept telling him her head hurt and all he did was bring her aspirin. Aspirin? He fluffed her off. Said everyone with a concussion gets a headache. I know he didn't call you to tell you."

Emily's face was wet with tears. "Please, let us take our daughter home."

"She's going to die just like my daughter did."

"But she had nothing to do with your wife or daughter's death. Neither did Damari Cooper. Why did you kill Damari?"

"That incompetent twit. We sat there at least an hour before she figured out the paperwork and got the insurance stuff together. Had she been quicker, Lisa would have lived."

Emily heard rustling at a quicker cadence than before. The voice seemed further away.

"I'm going to make good old Dr. Fox watch his wife and daughter die just like I watched mine. Only, he'll get to join his family. Consider it a present, not being left alive to deal with the pain."

The rustling increased. Dallas emerged from the corn, blocking their path. He held a shot gun. "Turn around. Keep walking."

Emily's mind worked into a frenzy. "If you take us in, the police can arrest Henry for what he did to your daughter. Trust me, jail would be worse than death. He'll pay the price for what he did to you."

"Oh, no. I've got a plan. Move." He poked her in the back with the shot gun. "Keep walking."

"Help me. Help."

"That's Maddy's voice. Where is she?" He smacked the gun against her cast, shooting pain up through her arm and into her neck. She grabbed her arm and said, "Maddy, we're here."

"Help me, please. He's crazy. He's going to kill me."

Her voice seemed closer. "We're here, Maddy."

"No one's going to hurt you, I swear on my life," said Henry.

They turned a corner and came to a clearing in the maze, with four paths shooting out in each direction. In the center, sat Maddy. Her hands and feet were tied with twine.

Emily ran to her. Henry followed.

"Get up," said Dallas. "Move away. The girl goes first." He aimed the shotgun and his finger wrapped over the trigger. Emily felt her heart beating like a jack hammer in her chest. This couldn't be the end. Not here in the middle of a corn maze. Not today.

Henry rushed into him, but Dallas was quick. He knocked him over the head with the gun, leaving him in an unconscious heap in the corn.

"Henry!" screamed Emily. Maddy just plain screamed.

Dallas kicked Henry. "Wake up. I want you to see this."

Henry moaned. His head felt like it had split into two throbbing knots. He fought to open his eyes. Dallas picked up the gun and aimed it at Maddy's head. "One, two..."

Emily cried, "No, please, no. Take me instead. Don't kill my daughter."

"Three."

Emily braced herself for the gun shot. She felt broken and helpless. She was supposed to protect Maddy. Fiona trusted her. She looked at Henry, who was still groggy and unable to get up.

"Take this you fool." From out of the corn, Robby stormed at him with a metal pipe and whacked him across the knees. Then he pulled Maddy to her feet and untied her. "Come on, let's get out of here before he can get up. Come on, Henry." He pulled Henry up and they ran down the closest path.

"You broke my kneecaps. You'll pay too!" He hugged his knees.

"Which way?" said Emily. They'd come to another crossroads.

"Follow me," said Robby.

Then they froze. A shot. Another shot."

"He's behind us; come on." Robby held onto Maddy. Henry struggled to keep up. He was seeing stars and imagined he had a concussion himself. The corn rustled. It was now dark as midnight and they felt their way along the path, barely lit by the sliver of moon above. Another shot pierced the darkness.

"I'm closing in on you. It's over Dr. Fox. You might as well surrender."

"This way," said Robby. They wound through the maze and came to a solid wall of corn.

"Now what?" said Emily. "There's no way out." If they ran back the way they came, surely they'd confront Dallas.

"I'm almost there." Dallas's voice was very near. Maddy was crying. Emily put her arm around her, heart breaking over her inability to protect her. Then, another shot. This time followed by a beam of light coming toward them.

"Megan! Ron Wooster!"

"We got him," said Megan. "Are you all okay?"

Henry was stumbling and grabbed Emily's arm for balance. "How did you find us?"

Megan pointed at Robby. "He's your hero. He called us."

"When I got to your house, I was just in time to see Dallas push Maddy into his van and speed away. I jumped back in my car and followed him. I called the police again when I knew the location."

Chapter 34

After giving a report to the police, they drove home, dropping an exhausted Robby off at the Inn. When they got back home, Maddy grabbed the mail on their way in.

Henry grabbed a bag of ice for his head and Emily took a warm shower. It was late, but she needed to be with her family. Henry and Maddy were eating cookies on the sofa when she made her way down the loft steps.

"Henry just filled me in on Charlie Rivers and the hidden fortune. I can't believe I missed all the excitement."

"Seriously? You didn't have enough excitement to last you at least a few weeks?"

"Guess you're right. Robby was a real hero. We wouldn't have made it if it wasn't for him."

"I approve," said Henry. "If you want to see this young man I'm okay with it."

Maddy laughed. "Like I need your approval."

Henry held his tongue. Emily changed the subject. "So any ideas about what to do with the money?"

Henry said, "I had a thought. It was a shame to see the old mill abandoned like that. Logging and running the mills is getting to be a lost art. What if we use the money to turn the mill into a museum? We could keep a piece of history alive."

"With all the visitors that pass through here, I think it'd be a hit."

"We could partner up with the guy at the corn maze and run a two for the price of one Vermont attraction ticket!"

Both Emily and Henry looked at her. "That's our girl," said Henry.

"I'm getting some almond milk to wash down these cookies," said Emily. "Anyone want some?"

"No thanks," said Henry.

"I still have some," said Maddy. Chester tried to stick his nose into her cup.

After she poured the milk, Emily picked up the mail that Maddy had left on the table.

"Maddy, there's a letter for you."

"For me?" She tore it open.

"Who's it from?" said Emily.

"You won't believe it. Listen to this.

*Dear Madelyn,*

*I'm hoping you are well. This will probably come as much as a surprise to you as it did to me. Last year a story broke in our local paper. A retired gynecologist was arrested for using his own sperm to impregnate patients, under the guise that he was using a sperm bank. Apparently, we have the same donor for a father. I had registered with Ancestors Are Us about a year ago, asking to flag any potential relatives. Guess what? You were a match. We're half-sisters. I'd love to meet you. I've enclosed my cell number and email. Hope to hear from you,*

*Sincerely,*

*Jessica Pratt.*

"I guess the excitement hasn't ended," said Emily.

"That's the company we used to trace your DNA. They keep a database," said Henry.

"Are you going to call her?" said Emily.

Maddy grabbed Chester and hugged him to her chest. "Hmm. Maybe I will."

# ABOUT THE AUTHOR

Diane Weiner is a veteran public school teacher and mother of four children. She has enjoyed reading for as long as she can remember. She has fond memories of reading Nancy Drew and Mary Higgins Clark on snowy weekend afternoons in upstate New York and yearned to write books that would bring that kind of enjoyment to her readers. Being an animal lover, she is a vegetarian and shares her home with two adorable cats. In her free time, she enjoys running, attending community theater productions, and spending time with her family (especially going to the mall with her teenage daughter and getting Dairy Queen afterwards).

*Clearing the Course,* is the third in Diane's Sugarbury Falls series. The first book in this series, *A Deadly Course*, recently received an Eric Hoffer International Book Competition Finalist Award for general fiction. The second is *Murder, of Course.*

Diane also writes the Susan Wiles Schoolhouse mysteries.

Visit dianeweinerauthor.com to find out more about the author.

# OTHER BOOKS BY DIANE WEINER

*Murder is Elementary*
*Murder is Secondary*
*Murder in the Middle*
*Murder is Private*
*Murder is Developmental*
*Murder is Legal*
*Murder is Collegiate*
*Murder is Chartered*
*Murder is Homework*

*A Deadly Course*
*Murder, of Course*

www.ingramcontent.com/pod-product-compliance
Lightning Source LLC
Chambersburg PA
CBHW020326260626
47156CB00004B/1389